HAMSTER PRINCESS

RATPUNZEL

HAMSTER PRINCESS

RATPUNZEL

BY
Ursula Vernon

SCHOLASTIC INC.

ISBN 978-1-338-22127-5

12 11 10 9 8 7 6 5 4 3 2 1   17 18 19 20 21 22

Printed in the U.S.A.   23

First Scholastic printing, October 2017

Design by Jennifer Kelly
Text set in Minister Std Light

For Kathy,
who, in a roundabout
fashion, was the
architect of my
success

CHAPTER 1

Harriet Hamsterbone had come home to her parents' castle, and she was already starting to regret it.

"Where have you been?" cried her mother, the queen, descending on her with a washcloth. "And how did you get so *grubby?*"

"I was saving princesses in the mouse kingdom," said Harriet, squirming away from the washcloth. She'd gotten home late and hadn't taken a bath before bed, but that was no reason to go flinging washcloths at her as if she were a little kid. "It was *important*."

"Saving princesses is all very good," said the queen, "but who's going to save you? You're not invincible anymore, dear."

"I'll save myself," said Harriet, puzzled. "That's why I've got a sword. And Mumfrey." (Mumfrey was her trusty battle quail.)

"Is it Tuesday?" asked the king, wandering into the room. "It feels like Tuesday . . ."

"It's Thursday, dear," said Harriet's mother, distracted.

"Are you sure?"

"Positive."

"Oh. Hmm. What happened to Wednesday?" Her father patted Harriet's shoulder absently. "Hello, honey. Did you have fun in the mouse kingdom?"

"I helped knock the mouse king's castle down," said Harriet, which was only a slight exaggeration.

The queen pressed a hand to her forehead. "*Harriet!* Did you apologize?"

"He was a bad king, Mom! He had gone to a very dark place in pursuit of organizational excellence!" (This was an understatement. The mouse king had been color-coding his guards and treating his daughters like a matched set. It had not gone well.)

"I suppose we can rule out getting a prince for you to marry from there," said her mother grimly. "Honestly, Harriet! You've terrified every eligible royal bachelor in ten kingdoms, and your room is a disaster."

"It can't be Thursday," said the king, winking at Harriet. "If it was Thursday, that would mean that we were having high tea with the Archbishop of Rodentbury, and I don't have any clean crowns."

The queen swung toward Harriet's father, her mouth falling open. "We are! In twenty minutes! I told you yesterday!"

"Is that what happened to Wednesday . . . ?"

The queen held the washcloth aloft. "You're coming with me!" she cried.

Harriet mouthed *thank you* silently to her father

as her mother dragged him
out of the room.

Harriet decided that maybe she'd been home
long enough. She grabbed a fresh change of
clothes from her dresser, raided the kitchen for
sandwich materials, and scurried down to the stables.

Mumfrey the quail poked his beak over the stall
door. He'd had a good meal of birdseed and was

ready to head back out again, if that's what his rider wanted.

Harriet led him out of the stables and through the gate, and swung herself up on quailback.

The castle shrank behind her.

"It's good to go home again," said Harriet. "If only so that you can *leave* home again."

"Qwerk."

After a while, as Mumfrey trotted along, Harriet started to sing.

IF I HAD A BROADSWORD, I'D SWING IT ALL OVER THIS LAND . . .

There are undoubtedly princesses out there with beautiful singing voices. Harriet was not one of them. She was good at hitting monsters with swords. Hitting *notes* was a little beyond her.

Mumfrey made it through twenty minutes of tuneless singing and was very glad when he saw someone in the distance.

The quail pointed one wing. Far down the road, a quailback rider was charging toward them.

"Oh," said Harriet. "Man, they're coming in fast too . . ."

She pulled Mumfrey's reins up and waited.

The rider did not slow down. If anything, he sped up.

"Hey, I think it's Wilbur!"

"Qwerk!"

It was indeed her friend Wilbur, a prince from the next kingdom over. He was bent low over the neck of his own riding quail, and his expression was grim.

He pulled up in front of Mumfrey and Harriet and practically fell out of the saddle. His quail, Hyacinth, dropped her head, panting.

"Jeez," said Harriet. "What's wrong? Is something on fire? Is your mother okay?"

"Harriet," gasped Wilbur. "You have to help." He staggered to Mumfrey's side and grabbed Harriet's ankle. "You have to help!"

"Of course I'll help," said Harriet. "What do you need me to do?"

"It's Heady," said Wilbur.

"Your hydra? What's wrong?"

"Her egg," he said. "It's been stolen."

Riding quails can't fly, but they can hop while flapping frantically. It's a good way to cover rough ground that they can't run over, because the quails' feet only touch the ground every few yards. This specialized gait is called "shlopping" and is well known among quail-riders everywhere.

If you are riding a quail who is shlopping, you cling to the reins as tightly as you can and try not to fall off. When the quail comes in for a landing, you stand in the stirrups so that you are not bounced brutally against the quail's back.

Above all else, you try not to think about how ridiculous you (and your quail) must look.

Wilbur and Harriet were taking the shortcut to Wilbur's mom's castle, which involved a lot of rocky terrain. Trying to run across it would have been dangerous for everyone involved, so they were shlopping.

Wilbur was not terribly good at it and kept missing the landings. He was looking a little seasick by the time the castle came into view.

It's very hard to communicate effectively while shlopping, so Harriet had not learned anything important, other than that the egg was missing and Heady the hydra was devastated.

"Why would anyone want to steal a hydra egg?" moaned Wilbur as they finally reached the road and settled into a more normal trot.

"Presumably they wanted a baby hydra," said Harriet. "Or a really big omelet, I guess . . ."

Wilbur shuddered. "Don't say anything about omelets to Heady! She's already upset!"

LAST NIGHT.
SHE HAS A NEST IN
THE BASEMENT. THIS
MORNING, WHEN WE
FINISHED BREAKFAST,
IT WAS GONE.

"Any chance that the egg could simply have been misplaced?"

Wilbur gave her a sideways look. "You've never seen a hydra egg, have you?"

Harriet had to admit that she had not.

"They're the size of a desk. It's not like you can just put one down for a minute and forget what you did with it."

"Right!" said Harriet. "I will investigate the scene of the crime! No one steals an innocent monster's egg on my watch!"

"Just . . . be nice to Heady," said Wilbur.

The castle that Wilbur's mother ran was small and rather run-down. The family fortunes had vanished long ago and left them with a castle that was expensive to keep up. Wilbur worked a variety of odd jobs to bring in money to fix the leaks in the roof.

Despite the disrepair, it was a cheerful little castle. Wilbur's mother was always cutting flowers in the meadow and arranging them in the hallways. It usually smelled like fresh-baked bread.

It was jarring to walk inside and hear loud sobbing from downstairs.

They left the quails in the courtyard and rushed down the steps to the basement, toward the sobbing sounds.

A hydra has nine snake-like heads, and every single one of Heady's was crying. Wilbur's mother

was holding tissues for one of the heads and saying "There, there," because that's the only thing to say when someone is crying. (Which is rather odd, when you think about it, because if you are crying because your egg has been stolen, "There, there" is much less helpful than "I've found your egg" or even "I will find your egg" or possibly "I will find those responsible for stealing your egg and beat them about the head and shoulders.")

"Oh, Heady!" said Wilbur. "It'll be okay! I brought Harriet!"

One head sniffled and turned toward the stairs.

"Harriet's going to get your egg back," said Wilbur. "You remember Harriet. She's invincible."

"Well, not any*more* . . ." said Harriet, but this didn't seem like the best time to get into the details.

Several more heads turned toward her.

"Can you show me where you saw the egg last?" asked Harriet.

Heady nodded and shuffled aside, leading the way into the back corner of the room.

The basement was warm and damp. Pipes zigzagged across the ceiling, dripping water onto the floor.

In the farthest corner, Heady had built a nest. It did not look like a bird nest built of twigs. Hydras are more like snakes or crocodiles, so Heady's nest was a lumpy mound, about knee high, and seemed to be made mostly of mud and old towels.

The hydra scuffed at the depression in the middle of the empty nest and let out another sob.

"She took *very* good care of the egg," said Wilbur's mother. "She checked on it every hour and she slept down here at night. I don't want you to think that Heady was careless in the least!"

"Nobody's saying that," said Harriet, patting one of the heads. "Heady's a *great* mom. When did the egg go missing?"

"Hisssss-sss-ssss," said Heady.

"Early in the morning," translated Wilbur.

"She got up to make breakfast and when she came back, the egg was gone," said Wilbur's mother. "Oh, you should see her make breakfast! Six heads with frying pans and three to crack the eggs. It's amazing."

Harriet nodded. She was familiar with Heady's astonishing cooking skills. "Anybody strange going in or out of the castle?"

MY DEAR HARRIET,
THERE'S ONLY FOUR OF US. WE
DON'T HAVE AN ARMY OF SERVANTS LIKE
YOU DO. IT'S ME AND WILBUR AND
HEADY AND THE GARDENER.

OH. UM.
RIGHT. WELL,
THAT NARROWS
IT DOWN.

"You can't think it was the
gardener," said Wilbur's mother. "He's ninety years
old and the only thing he cares about is plants."

"Are you sure?" asked Harriet. "No secret egg-
smuggling rings?"

HE GETS VERY
WORKED UP OVER OKRA AND
THEN HE HAS TO SIT DOWN FOR
TEN MINUTES. I DON'T THINK
HE TOOK THE EGG.

Harriet had to admit that it seemed unlikely. She stared at the muddy nest.

It wasn't a very pretty nest. It wasn't the sort of place where you'd expect to find something valuable. In fact, if you were looking for something valuable, you probably wouldn't go looking in Wilbur's castle in the first place.

"They knew the egg was here," said Harriet slowly. "It wasn't random. They didn't just break in looking for stuff. Whoever took it must have *known* you had a hydra egg." She crouched down in front of the nest, looking closely at the mud.

"It's not like Heady's a secret," said Wilbur's mother. She patted the hydra.

SHE'S A MEMBER OF THE FAMILY.

"Hiss-sss-ss," said Heady sadly. One of her other heads teared up again.

"But who would have done this?" asked Wilbur, wringing his hands.

"I don't know," said Harriet, standing up. "And I don't know where they've gone or how they got in undetected."

She pointed at one corner of the nest. "But I *do* know that they left a footprint."

CHAPTER 2

The print was longer than Harriet's foot, but a lot narrower. "Gerbil, I think," said Harriet. "If I'm right—ha! Yes, here's the tail print. You can see where the hairs were in the mud."

"That rules out the gardener," said Wilbur. "And anybody in the castle."

His mother frowned. "I've got a few friends who are gerbils," she said, "but they're all pen pals now. They haven't even been to visit in years."

"Have you written to any of them recently?" asked Harriet. "And if so, did you mention the egg?"

Wilbur's mother tapped one of her nails against her teeth. "Hmm . . ."

"I don't know," said the older hamster. "She's a lovely woman, really. Very into plants. A little hard to get along with sometimes, but I can't think that she would steal Heady's egg."

"Lots of us have friends who are hard to get along with sometimes," muttered Wilbur, giving Harriet a meaningful look.

"Huh?" said Harriet.

". . . never mind," said Wilbur. His mother chuckled.

"Anyway, maybe she didn't steal the egg. Maybe she just left the letter lying around and someone read it. It can't hurt to check it out."

"All right," said Wilbur's mother. "I've got her reply around here somewhere. Let's check the return address and see what we've got."

They tromped upstairs, after reassuring Heady that they were hot on the trail of the missing egg.

Harriet's last view of the disconsolate hydra was a tangle of heads curling up around the nest and sighing heavily.

"Poor Heady," she said once they reached the courtyard. "I didn't know she'd feel that way about her egg. Quails don't get nearly so attached to their eggs." She considered this. "Of course, they also have a bunch at a time . . ."

"Hydras only have one," said Wilbur's mother. "She's so maternal. She mothers all of us, and she was so excited to have her own egg. It breaks your heart to see it."

The study was a disaster. Papers were piled on every surface, including the floor and the chairs. Wilbur and Harriet stood around with their hands in their pockets, waiting, while Wilbur's mother dug through her big rolltop desk.

Harriet took the envelope and read the return address. "Dame Gothel . . . Deadly Tower . . ."

"That sounds ominous!" said Wilbur.

". . . Tiddlywinks Lane . . ."

"That sounds . . . less ominous?"

". . . Forest of Misery . . ."

"More ominous!"

". . . Kingdom of Sunshine."

"Yeah, I give up," said Wilbur.

"She's really very sweet," said his mother, opening the letter. "Listen to this . . ."

My dear Hazel,

It is so sweet of you to write. I do enjoy hearing about the goings-on in the wide world. I spend so much time here in my tower, with my plants, that I rarely travel as widely as I would like. You always tell me about such unusual things! A hydra who cooks! And she had an egg? Perhaps I should come visit you someday soon. Please do tell me more, and know how much I treasure your letters.

Hugs,
Gothel

Harriet frowned. On the surface, the letter didn't seem that strange. But it was clear that Gothel knew about the egg, and that was something.

She tapped the envelope. "Well, it's the only lead we've got. Let's go talk to Dame Gothel."

CHAPTER 3

Harriet and Wilbur rode toward the address listed on the envelope, arguing as they went.

"This is very simple," said Harriet. "We will find Dame Gothel and I will point my sword at her and say, 'Tell us everything you know about the hydra egg.'"

VIOLENCE ISN'T THE ANSWER, HARRIET!

"Violence is a *great* answer. I have personally answered twenty-eight Ogrecats with violence! And they are all reformed characters now too. Two of them make baby clothes for disadvantaged guinea pigs."

Wilbur clutched his head. Harriet had a very direct personality. Sometimes a little *too* direct.

"Violence should always be the last resort. We should *talk* to Dame Gothel first."

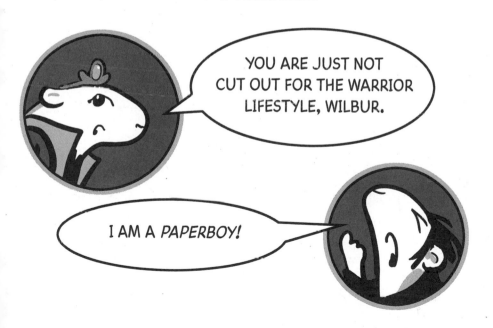

YOU ARE JUST NOT CUT OUT FOR THE WARRIOR LIFESTYLE, WILBUR.

I AM A *PAPERBOY!*

"Anyway," said Wilbur, "we are not going to attack an innocent gerbil—who happens to be a friend of my *mom's*—just because she got a letter about the egg!" He sniffed. "We'll ask her, first, if she's seen the egg."

Harriet grumbled. "Fine," she said. "Heady's your hydra. We'll do it your way."

"Thank you."

". . . for now."

"Qwerk," said Hyacinth the quail, sounding amused.

"Qwerk," agreed Mumfrey.

"I heard that," said Harriet.

The Kingdom of Sunshine was a few days away by quail. They slept on the ground, which Harriet was used to and Wilbur hated.

"Are you kidding?" said Harriet. "The Land of Comfortable Beds is terrifying. Monsters under *everything*."

Everyone in the Kingdom of Sunshine was cheerful, in that extremely grating way that made your teeth ache.

"Isn't it a magnificent day?!" asked a farmer, leaning on his hoe by the side of the road.

"Don't you just want to hug the clouds today?" asked a flower-seller in the town square.

"It's going to be the best day ever!" shouted a little girl, running by with a doll behind her.

WE'RE GOING TO HAVE THE BEST TEA PARTY THAT EVER WAS, MR. WIGGLES!

"Everyone seems very . . . happy . . ." said Wilbur.

"Yep," said Harriet. "Not gonna lie. If I had to live here, I'd go evil in a week. I'd be building an army of giant spider-chickens and saying things like, 'No, Mr. Wilbur, I expect you to die, muaha-haha.'"

"Qwerkahahaha!" said Mumfrey, with feeling.

"Yes, exactly like that."

"You're just cynical, Harriet."

"Let's see how you feel in another day or two. We're only two-fifths of the way across the king-dom."

Wilbur rolled his eyes. Harriet had a strange ob-session with fractions, but there was no point in trying to get her to drop it. "Everyone should be happy," he said instead.

"Yes, but they don't have to be obnoxious about it."

They stopped at an inn for lunch. The inn-keeper told them at length about how the King-dom of Sunshine was the happiest kingdom, and how thrilled he was to live there and how his grandchildren made him confident in the future of rodentkind.

Harriet interrupted his monologue to ask if he had seen a gerbil with a giant egg.

"Not with an egg, no," said the innkeeper. "And this is my granddaughter when she was a year old . . ."

"Without an egg, then?" asked Harriet.

"Look at that face! And here she is when she was two years old. . . . Oh, yes. A gerbil lady in a cloak. She came and bought sausages and left. Now, here I have a poem that my granddaughter wrote about clouds . . ."

DID SHE SAY ANYTHING ABOUT WHERE SHE WAS GOING?

"O cloud! You make the sun so happy, my heart overflows with love—"

Harriet gritted her teeth. She didn't think she could handle happy poetry.

"Please," said Wilbur, "it's kind of important. Did the gerbil lady say anything?"

The innkeeper paused in his recitation. "The poem won an award," he said. "Most Joyful Poem About Weather in the Third Grade."

"Lives may be at stake," said Wilbur.

"Oh my! Well, no. Just that she couldn't ever get good cooking at home. Said her taste buds were positively withering away. They were lovely sausages."

"Thank you," said Wilbur.

"My other granddaughter wrote a sonnet about sausages. It was voted Most Joyful Poem About Meat Products in the Second Grade. I could recite it for you, if you like."

GREAT SAUSAGE! MIGHTY QUEEN OF MEATS! YOU ARE—

"Perhaps another time," said Wilbur. One of Harriet's eyelids was twitching. They left the inn in a hurry.

"Well," said Wilbur. "If that was her, she came by here. But she didn't have the egg."

"You wouldn't take the egg into an inn," said Harriet. "People'd notice a giant egg. Around here, they'd probably compose poems about it."

They stayed at an inn that night. The inn had featherbeds. The innkeeper confirmed that a gerbil had come through several days earlier, gotten food, and left again, and that she had spent ten minutes talking about how dreadful the cooking was at home.

"She was very negative," said the innkeeper. "I felt just terrible for her. I sang her a song to cheer her up."

"I sang 'I'm So Happy, I Could Hug the World' and 'A Smile Is a Dream Written on Your Face' and—"

"Which way did she go?" asked Wilbur. He still sounded pleasant, but Harriet could hear him grinding his teeth.

The innkeeper pointed down the road, in the direction of the Forest of Misery. "Would you like me to sing?"

"*No!*" said Wilbur quickly. "That's fine!" They fled the inn.

"I am beginning to see your point," said Wilbur an hour later as they climbed the steps to the bedrooms. "I mean, I get that he likes to sing, but 'The Happy Bluebird Is So Happy, He Makes Me Happy Too' was a bit much. They're all very nice people, they're just a little . . . *too* happy."

"Muahaha!" said Harriet.

By the time they came to the Forest of Misery, it was almost a relief.

"Dark, dank, dripping," said Harriet. "No songs about happiness. No poems about meat products. I could get to like this place."

"What I'm wondering is why they called it the Forest of Misery," said Wilbur. "You have to think that in a place like the Kingdom of Sunshine, they'd have a happier name for it. Like . . . oh . . . I dunno . . ."

"It's a bit long," said Wilbur. "I was thinking the Forest That Just Needs a Nap, or something."

"Qwerk-erk!"

"That's a good one too."

The trees clutched at them with dark, twiggy fingers as they rode past. Moss dripped from trunks and spread a thick green carpet over the ground. Pale mushrooms glowed underneath the trees.

Somewhere, a bird called in a low, mournful voice, like a flute being played at a funeral.

"Cheery," said Wilbur.

"Still better than the Kingdom of Sunshine."

"I feel like something's watching us," said Wilbur.

"Yep," said Harriet.

"You feel it too?"

"Yeah."

"Probably my nerves."

"Well, that and the pack of weasel-wolves that's been following us."

"Weasel-wolves?" squeaked Wilbur.

"For about the last half mile," said Harriet. She drew her sword. "Don't panic. They won't attack unless they think we're an easy target."

Wilbur thought about this for a minute.

"Err . . . Harriet?"

"Yes?"

". . . we *are* an easy target."

"Speak for yourself!" said Harriet, and then the weasel-wolves attacked.

Harriet saw the first weasel-wolf break from the undergrowth and launch itself at Hyacinth.

It was a blur of teeth and claws and tail, and it was extremely fast.

Mumfrey, however, was faster.

Harriet's trusty battle quail lunged between Hyacinth and the monster. The weasel-wolf suddenly discovered that it was no longer charging at a panicked target, but at Harriet Hamsterbone, notorious monster slayer.

Harriet grinned.

She didn't even have to do anything. She just held her sword up and the weasel-wolf's jump carried it right into the pommel, cracking itself in the forehead. Its eyes crossed and it fell to the ground, where Mumfrey stepped on it a few times for good measure.

Another weasel-wolf charged. Hyacinth leaped straight into the air, shlopping frantically, and her attacker fell back with a mouthful of tail feathers. Mumfrey squawked with rage. Hyacinth was his girlfriend!

He spun around—Harriet grabbed for the reins—so that his rump was facing the startled weasel-wolf. The monster spat out the feathers and grinned.

What it did not know was that the most dangerous place you can be is directly *behind* a battle quail.

Mumfrey's power was all in his kick. His legs shot out—one-two—and lifted the weasel-wolf off its feet. It flew through the air, bounced off a tree trunk, and ran into the woods with its tail between its stubby legs.

"Qwerk!" said Mumfrey, which is Quail for "Hmmph!"

The weasel-wolves looked at her, looked at one another, and melted away into the forest. Harriet sheathed her sword.

"That's that," she said. "They're cowards."

Wilbur slid off Hyacinth's back. "You're the best quail," he told her. "You don't have to be scared. You did great!"

Mumfrey looked vaguely offended. He'd done all the work! But Harriet patted his neck. She knew that Hyacinth wasn't a battle quail the way that Mumfrey was, and she needed to be reassured after the encounter.

"You shlopped at just the right time," said Harriet to Hyacinth. "That was perfect!"

Hyacinth made a small, fretful *qwerk* but straightened up. She settled her feathers a bit.

"Let's keep moving," said Harriet. "We've still got to find this tower. On . . . err . . ." She checked the envelope. ". . . Tiddlywinks Lane."

They rode on through the Forest of Misery. Occasionally Harriet would spot a weasel-wolf out of the corner of her eye, but they looked less like hunters and more like prey.

And then the road they were on branched. The main thoroughfare continued on, but to one side, an even darker and more forbidding pathway beckoned.

There was a cheerful signpost at the fork, looking wildly out of place. Harriet got off Mumfrey to go and read it.

"That doesn't look happy," said Wilbur. "That looks like the opposite of happy."

"Sad?"

"Painful!"

"Still," said Harriet. "I guess this is the way we're supposed to go . . ."

A cold breeze blew through the Forest of Misery. Wilbur wrapped his arms around himself and shuddered.

CHAPTER 4

They had to ride single file down Tiddlywinks Lane. Harriet took the lead.

Around them, the Forest of Misery dripped and squished and groaned.

"This is starting to get to me," said Wilbur. "I mean, it's like it's being deliberately unpleasant. Look at that tree there." He pointed. "It's totally got angry faces in it. And so does that one. *And* that one."

Harriet peered at one of the trees. It did indeed seem to have a rodent face in it.

"That's weird," she said. "Normally those things are just tricks of the eye, but that looks like an actual person in that tree."

"And that one over there too," said Wilbur. "And that other one. And . . . hmm."

Harriet tapped her claw against her big front teeth. "That one looks like a quail."

"Qwerk!"

She slid off Mumfrey's back and walked a little way into the forest. Most of the trees in every direction looked as if the bark had been carved into the shapes of people.

"There's a newt," she said. "And that thicket there is like a dozen weasel-wolves."

The resemblance was uncanny. A few of the faces did look angry, but most of them just looked puzzled. One or two looked surprised.

"Maybe Dame Gothel likes to carve," said Wilbur.

"Sure," said Harriet. "That's definitely the most likely possibility."

"Right," said Wilbur.

"And we don't know that it's Gothel doing . . . whatever this is," said Harriet, climbing back onto Mumfrey. "Although didn't your mom say that she was very into plants?"

"I thought she meant that Gothel . . . oh, grew roses or prize-winning zucchini or something." Wilbur ducked under a branch that grew over

the path. It looked alarmingly like a warrior rat holding up a spear.

"I suppose that's possible."

They rode on. More carved tree trunks appeared on either side. Most were carvings of people, with scattered beasts and birds among them. One massive oak tree was carved into the shape of a crouching Ogrecat. Harriet got down again and walked around that one.

"It's frighteningly good," said Harriet. "With the emphasis on *frightening*. It's got whiskers, and the tail's just right too."

"I don't like this," said Wilbur.

"We're here for Heady's egg," said Harriet. "Just remember that."

They passed more trees. Most of them looked like people, except for the ones that looked like ordinary trees.

A couple, though . . .

"That's weird," said Harriet.

One of the trees looked mostly like a tree, except that there was an enormous slash in the trunk. It gaped open like a mouth, and Harriet could see heartwood inside.

The tree looked as if it should be dead, with that kind of opening in it, but it had leafed out and appeared completely healthy.

"Really weird," said Wilbur. "Can we get back on the quail now?"

"Yeah," said Harriet. "Yeah . . ."

They rode onward.

They hadn't gone more than a few dozen yards when Mumfrey halted, flipping his topknot nervously.

"What is it?"

"Qwerk!" said Mumfrey, which is Quail for "Someone in the road."

Harriet slid off the quail's back and advanced. She could see what he was looking at—a long, rope-like thing lying across the road.

It was an awfully shaggy rope, though. And there was a black tip on the end.

"Come out!" yelled Harriet. "I know you're there!"

"How do you know that?" said the bushes.

"Because your tail is sticking out!"

With rustling and rattling and thumping and a great deal of noise, an elderly gerbil in a black cloak slowly emerged from the bushes.

"Oh, dearie me," said the gerbil. "Dearie me. I'm sorry, I thought you were weasel-wolves."

"Uh-huh," said Harriet. "Are you Dame Go-thel?"

The gerbil's eyes went sharp for an instant, then softened, so quickly that Harriet wasn't sure if she'd seen it at all. "Why, yes, my dear. Do I know you?"

"You're friends with my mom," said Wilbur. "I'm Wilbur."

"Oh! Yes, of course, Hazel's little boy! Why, how nice to see you! She writes about you all the time." Dame Gothel clasped her hands together. "Such a good, sweet boy! She's so proud of you."

Wilbur blushed and mumbled something.

AND YOU MUST BE . . . ?

PRINCESS HARRIET HAMSTERBONE.

WELL, SHE HASN'T MENTIONED YOU, BUT I'M SURE YOU'RE A GOOD, SWEET GIRL TOO!

Harriet opened her mouth to say something— probably not something terribly good or sweet— and Wilbur hastily said, "We're looking for a stolen hydra egg!"

Harriet closed her mouth again and glared at Wilbur. If Gothel was the egg thief, blurting it out wasn't going to make their job any easier.

That odd expression flicked across the gerbil's face again. Harriet studied her closely, frowning a little. Gothel didn't seem to have the egg . . . but something didn't add up.

"A hydra egg?" said Gothel. "Dear me! I've never seen a hydra. They're supposed to be naturally gifted cooks, though."

"Heady is," said Wilbur. "She's brilliant. But someone took her egg."

"Oh, the poor thing!" Gothel clasped her wrist to her forehead. "Oh, there's such wickedness in the world."

"We thought you might have heard about it, since my mom wrote you . . ."

"Oh, no, my dear sweet boy." Gothel patted his hand. "I don't think she said anything about an egg, no. Not to me."

"So you *haven't* seen the egg," said Harriet.

THE LAST EGG
I SAW HAD BEEN
POACHED. AT LEAST, SHE
SAID IT WAS POACHED.
IT LOOKED LIKE A LITTLE
YELLOW BRICK AND SHE'D
DUMPED SEA SALT AND
ANCHOVIES ON IT.

The gerbil shuddered theatrically.

"So is your tower around here?" asked Wilbur.

"No," said Gothel. "Not anywhere nearby."

"I thought this was Tiddlywinks Lane."

"Oh, well, yes. It is. But it goes on for a long way. Miles. Days of travel. Anyway, I should get moving if I'm going to get home. It was lovely to meet you!"

There was an awkward silence. Gothel stood in the middle of the path and didn't move.

"Right," said Harriet. "Sorry to bother you. We were hoping you'd seen it. Come on, Wilbur, let's ride away from here and see if we can find the thief somewhere . . . else. Far away. Now."

Wilbur blinked at her. Harriet jerked her head toward the quails.

"Right," said Wilbur. "Uh . . . thanks, ma'am. It was nice meeting you."

"You're so sweet! I shall write your mother and tell her that you are a delightful young man, young man."

Gothel waved. Harriet turned Mumfrey and broke into a fast quail trot.

"That was odd," said Wilbur, when they were out of earshot.

"That was *beyond* odd," said Harriet. "She was

lying about your mother mentioning the egg in her letters, did you notice?"

SHE COULD HAVE JUST FORGOTTEN, I GUESS . . .

Harriet urged Mumfrey off the path, into the woods. "Come on. She's probably waiting to make sure we're gone. I want to circle around ahead of her and see where this tower is."

"She said it was days away," said Wilbur, following.

"Yeah," said Harriet. "Did you believe her?"

Wilbur shook his head slowly. "No."

ME NEITHER. AND I WANT TO FIND OUT WHAT'S GOING ON.

CHAPTER 5

The woods were deep, and full of unpleasant carvings. Harriet focused on moving quietly. In this, Hyacinth was better than Mumfrey. She was light on her feet and could hop delicately over dry branches that a heavy battle quail would just stomp through.

They halted every few minutes to listen. Unfortunately, it's hard to hear a gerbil walking down a path hundreds of yards away when you are crashing through the trees with a pair of quails. Harriet settled for just trying to go in the right direction.

After a few more minutes, the woods suddenly opened up. Light poured in from overhead.

They had reached a clearing. Off to their left, Tiddlywinks Lane ran forward, zigzagging back and forth, and finally ended at the base of a tower.

"Oh, look," said Harriet. "An enchanted tower covered in thorns. Not *again!*"

Princesses and towers go together. Everybody knows this. Even people who have never seen a tower or met a princess will instinctively feel that if you've got one, you have to have the other.

This has something to do with the sorts of books that people read, but also something to do with witches and wizards and fairies. Most magical folk like that are great traditionalists. If they are going to imprison a princess, they will automatically reach for a tower, instead of, say, a hole

in the ground lined with spikes.

Harriet had mixed feelings about this. On the one hand, she herself had once had a tower, which had been over-grown with thorn bushes. She was not terribly keen on them as a result. After the incident, she'd moved down into the main body of the castle, and the tower was now a guest bedroom.

On the other hand, a hole in the ground lined with spikes rarely has much of a view.

It wasn't a bad tower. It went straight up and had a little round roof and two large windows. The base was wrapped in gigantic thorns, except for one tiny clear patch directly under the window.

There were no doors that Harriet could see, but there was a mailbox.

It had a pattern of leaves on it and read, in cheerful letters, "Deadly Tower."

"This is weird, right?" said Wilbur. "It's not just me."

"It's a little odd," said Harriet. "In fact, I could go so far as peculiar."

"And it was less than a mile away."

Harriet nodded.

"Maybe we should—"

"Hsst!" Harriet held up a hand. "Someone's coming!"

It's fairly easy to hide a hamster in the woods, but much more difficult to hide a pair of riding quails. Mumfrey and Hyacinth hurried deeper into the woods together, while Harriet and Wilbur squeezed behind trees.

Gothel came hurrying down the path, into the clearing. She was bent nearly double . . . because she was carrying an enormous egg in a rope harness on her back. Harriet realized the cloak must have somehow been hiding the egg before.

"That's—!" Wilbur began, outraged.

Harriet slapped her paw over his mouth.

"—mmmf!"

"I know," whispered the hamster warrior, "but keep quiet! We don't want her to know we're here!"

"Go get her!" hissed Wilbur in her ear, when she let him talk. "Get it back! That belongs to Heady!"

"Yes, it does," Harriet whispered back. "But she's a witch!"

Wilbur paused. "How do you know?"

"Look at the size of that egg! Do you think an ordinary old woman is carrying an egg bigger than she is? And how did we not see it in the bushes earlier? She's done some kind of magic to it!"

"All right, fine, she's a witch! But you've fought witches! Go fight this one!"

Harriet shook her head. There was nothing inherently wrong with being a witch. (Harriet would have quite liked to be one herself, but she didn't seem to have the knack for it.) Some witches were good, some were bad. All of them were powerful.

The problem was that you generally wanted to know what sort of powers they had before you started waving a sword around. It was one thing to challenge a witch who could tell the future, and quite another to challenge a witch whose hobby was turning people into earwigs.

Harriet was getting a particularly bad feeling about those carvings.

"Just wait," she whispered to Wilbur. "We know where the egg is and where she lives. If I rush in now, there's a chance the egg will get broken."

Wilbur blinked, but subsided. Harriet could feel him vibrating with outrage next to her.

She couldn't blame him. It was Heady's egg, after all, and Wilbur loved Heady. Harriet was very fond of Heady too, but she was a warrior, and good warriors knew when to rush in with swords and when to wait and get a feel for the lay of the land. She hadn't saved the mouse princesses by charging in and smacking everyone in the palace with her blade, even if she'd been pretty tempted at the time.

The old gerbil looked around suspiciously. Her eyes moved over the trees. Harriet shoved Wilbur out of sight and held perfectly still.

After a minute, Gothel seemed to relax. She walked across the clearing, to the base of the tower.

RATPUNZEL, RATPUNZEL! LET DOWN YOUR TAIL!

Someone appeared at the window. Harriet was too far away to make out many details, but something like a rope dropped down the side of the tower.

Gothel hitched up the egg, grabbed the rope, and began to climb.

That's weird, Harriet thought. *Ropes aren't usually pink.*

Harriet watched until she vanished over the windowsill. The odd rope was pulled back up.

She leaned back against the tree trunk and let out a long sigh.

"What's happening?" whispered Wilbur. "Is the egg okay?!"

"The egg's fine," said Harriet. "But things just got *very* weird."

CHAPTER 6

Wilbur and Harriet retreated into the forest. Mumfrey qwerked at them, and led them to a small, protected clearing, out of sight of the tower.

There was a weirdly carved tree there, but only one and it wasn't looking at them. It looked like a handsome rat prince, holding a shield and a sword.

"Good armor," said Harriet, tapping one of the rat's shoulder guards. "High-quality . . . um . . . bark."

"Well, it's only a carving," said Wilbur.

"Sure," said Harriet. "Let's just keep pretending that for now, shall we?"

Wilbur winced. "Are you sure they couldn't . . . just . . . ?" He gesture aimlessly at the forest, and the rather terrifying number of people-like trees.

Harriet sighed.

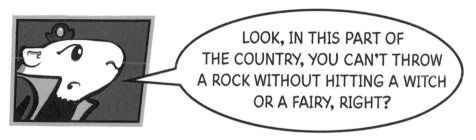

AND MOST OF THEM ARE VERY GOOD PEOPLE! NO MORE THAN TEN PERCENT EVIL MAGICIANS, TOPS!

"Whereas I've met like three sculptors in my entire life," Harriet continued, "and none of them were evil. I mean, one of them couldn't remember if he was wearing pants most days, but not evil." She held up her paws. "So that means we've got one-tenth of magicky people being bad, versus zero out of three, which is no-thirds, because if you've got a zero on top of a fraction . . ."

"I get it!" yelled Wilbur. "I'm trying to stay in denial here, okay?!"

Harriet patted his shoulder. "It's all right," she said. "The important thing is that the egg is safe for now."

"How do you know that!?" asked Wilbur.

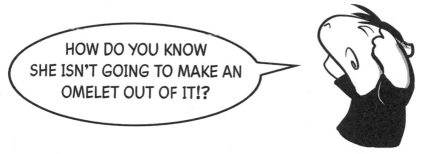

HOW DO YOU KNOW SHE ISN'T GOING TO MAKE AN OMELET OUT OF IT!?

"Most people don't travel for days carrying a giant egg so they can make an omelet," said Harriet. "I mean, you have to really *want* that omelet."

"Most people don't live in the Deadly Tower in the Forest of Misery either!"

"I'm sure it'll be fine," said Harriet soothingly. "For now, let's set up a camp here, and then go spy on the tower. I want to try something when Gothel leaves."

Wilbur sighed. He couldn't very well go and storm the tower by himself. "Fine," he said. "We'll do it your way."

They left the quails settled in the clearing and crept back toward the tower.

They didn't have to wait for long. Well . . . long by the standards of a hamster warrior patiently stalking her prey. By Wilbur's standards, it was more than long enough.

"My foot's asleep!"

"Hush! You want her to hear us?"

"I think my tail's asleep too!"

"Just wiggle your toes," whispered Harriet. "And—shhh! Here she comes!"

The odd pink rope fell back out of the window. Gothel, no longer carrying the egg, climbed down it. Whoever was at the top pulled the rope back up as soon as she reached the bottom.

She did not look around this time, but hurried down the path and into the forest.

"Where's she going?" whispered Wilbur.

"No idea," said Harriet. "But there's not a lot to do in the forest, so hopefully she's at least going outside it. This is our chance!"

She darted out of the woods toward the tower.

Wilbur followed, looking over his shoulder. "Do you know how to get into the tower?"

Harriet took a deep breath. "We'll find out . . ." she muttered.

She made her way carefully through the break in the thorns, to the clear patch at the base of the tower. Wilbur followed her.

The tower looked very solid. There was no trace of a door in the wall facing them, and no handholds.

Just under the window, there was an odd little bar.

Harriet cleared her throat and called, "Ratpunzel, Ratpunzel! Let down your tail!"

Wilbur stared at her as if she'd lost her mind.

"What was that supposed to be?" he asked, and then something fell out of the sky and whacked him over the head.

CHAPTER 7

It was a tail.

In fact, it was a rat tail, although it was about fifty times longer than any tail that Harriet had ever seen on a rat. It was long and pink and resembled a rather rugged earthworm.

"Ow!" said Wilbur, rubbing his head.

The owner of the tail had looped it around the bar under the window and was looking down. From this distance, Harriet couldn't see much, except that she appeared to be a rather young rat.

"Hello?" called the rat. "Do I know you?"

"I'm Harriet Hamsterbone," said Harriet. "May I come up?"

"Sure!"

Harriet rubbed her hands together and began hauling herself up the freakishly long tail.

It was a long climb, but Harriet had the sort of muscles you get from swinging a

sword and hitting ogres over the head. Wilbur came up behind her. He had the sort of muscles you get from being a paperboy, which were less impressive, but since he also shoveled a lot of stables, he wasn't a weakling.

When Harriet reached the window, the young rat maiden helped her over the windowsill.

They both hauled Wilbur into the tower. Harriet looked around.

The tower had a large central room, with a small ladder leading up to a loft and a set of stairs leading down. There was a brightly colored rug on the floor, and the walls were painted a cheerful yellow.

Heady's egg was nowhere in sight.

"Did . . . um . . . a gerbil come here earlier?" asked Harriet. "With an egg?"

"Mother Gothel, yes," said Ratpunzel. She twisted her tail in her hands. "Such a big egg! She took it downstairs."

"To the kitchen?" asked Wilbur faintly.

"Don't be silly," said Ratpunzel. "It's not an *eating* egg. Although I bet I could make an amazing frittata out of it. With bell peppers and trout flakes!"

"Nobody's making frittatas out of that egg!" cried Wilbur.

Ratpunzel blinked. "It's all right," she said hurriedly, patting his arm. "I won't. It's obviously a very special egg. Even I can see that, and I've never been out of this tower."

"What, never?" asked Harriet, startled.

"Mother Gothel says it's very dangerous out there. Full of monsters." She looked at Harriet thoughtfully. "Are you a monster?"

DEPENDS ON WHO YOU ASK.

WILBUR! NOT HELPFUL!

"I'm *not* a monster," said Harriet. "Monsters are afraid of me."

"You do look very fierce," said Ratpunzel. "I can see why monsters don't bother you." She looked at Wilbur. "You don't look quite so fierce . . ."

"I'm not," said Wilbur. "I'm a paperboy."

ARE YOU MADE OF PAPER? YOU LOOK VERY FURRY . . .

UH . . . NO. I DELIVER PAPERS. NOT THE SAME.

"Oh. That sounds interesting!"

"Um . . ." Wilbur threw Harriet a pleading look. "Not *that* interesting . . ."

"I'm sure it's fascinating!" said Ratpunzel. "Do you get to go outside?"

"Lots," said Wilbur. "All over."

Ratpunzel clasped her hands together. "What's it like outside?"

"Oh, you know . . ." said Harriet. "Lots of stuff . . . like . . . um . . . the entire world . . ." She was drawing a bit of a blank. How did you explain the world to someone who'd spent their whole life in a tower?

"I've seen a lot out the window," said Ratpunzel. "I wish there was another window on the other side, though. I only ever see the sun set. I've never seen it rise."

"It's pretty much the same, only backward," said

Harriet. "Less reddish, more . . . um . . . grayish bluish."

"I wish I could see it," said Ratpunzel wistfully.

"So why don't you?" asked Harriet. "Can't you get out of the tower?"

Ratpunzel finished pulling her tail up and wrapped it around her arm like a coil of rope. "Well . . . I mean, I could probably climb down my own tail . . ."

"Doesn't that hurt?" asked Wilbur. "I mean, when people climb up your tail?" He poked his own small stub of a tail. "There's little tiny bones in it, aren't there?"

THREE HUNDRED AND EIGHTY-SEVEN BONES! I COUNTED. BUT IT'S MAGIC, SO IT DOESN'T HURT AT ALL.

She thumped her tail with her hand. "Actually, I can hardly feel anything on it. And it's super-sturdy."

Her tail wiggled a bit, as if it appreciated the praise. She patted it. It was cute, and just slightly creepy.

"Maybe you got a lot of extra bones and no extra nerves," said Wilbur.

"So why don't you leave?" asked Harriet.

"Mother Gothel told me not to," said Ratpunzel. "And if I climb down, I can't get back up, and neither can she. We'd be stuck. There aren't any doors. My tail is the only way into the tower."

CHAPTER 8

*W*ell, Harriet thought that night as she curled up under Mumfrey's wing. *Well.*

That had certainly been . . . interesting.

Ratpunzel had been very excited to talk about the outside world. She was particularly interested in what they ate. Wilbur told Ratpunzel all about what they'd had for breakfast while Harriet poked around the tower.

She hadn't gone into Gothel's bedroom. Rat-punzel had said "I'm not allowed in there," and it had seemed rude to simply open the door in front of her. But she'd inspected the kitchen (which was a perfectly ordinary kitchen, with a well-stocked pantry) and the main room, and Ratpunzel's bedroom upstairs.

Ratpunzel passed the time by cooking. She had a mountain of cookbooks nearly six feet high.

"I've cooked every recipe in the books!" she said happily. "Mother Gothel keeps bringing me ingredients. She says she's hoping I'll get a good one, but I think the key is improvisation! A great chef knows how to make any dish her own!"

She flung her arms wide. "Someday I shall have a restaurant in the tower and people will come from miles around to sample my fish-flake ice cream!"

"Fish-flake ice cream . . . ?"

"I haven't worked all the kinks out yet. You need peppercorns. And squid ink. Mother Gothel won't bring me any more squid ink. She says fish ice cream is an abomination."

Wilbur looked as if he might have just found something in common with Mother Gothel.

Harriet, meanwhile, had been staring at the sheer *size* of the pile and thinking about how long it would take and how Ratpunzel must have been cooking recipes all day, every day, for years and years . . .

"We've got to get you out of this tower," she blurted.

"Oh, I'd like that," said Ratpunzel. "But I don't expect it. I mean, the prince said he could do that, and . . . well . . ."

"Prince?" said Wilbur. "What prince?"

THE NICE PRINCE. HE CAME BY AND TALKED TO ME, AND I LIKED HIM VERY MUCH AND I COOKED MY VERY BEST ASPARAGUS WAFFLES FOR HIM, BUT THEN HE STOPPED COMING.

"Mother Gothel didn't like it when she found him here," she added. "But then she carved a tree to look like him, so I wouldn't be sad. So I guess she forgave him!"

Wilbur and Harriet turned their heads very slowly and looked at each other.

There are times when two friends can communicate entirely without talking, and what they said to each other was, *Are you thinking what I'm thinking?*

Oh yeah.

That's not a carving.

Nope.

This is awful.

Yep.

Wilbur had to pause, because Harriet was doing a thing with her eyebrow that was either *Let's just burn everything down* or *I could really go for a churro about now,* and neither one seemed quite right.

"Well," he said, in a rather horrible trying-to-be-cheerful voice, "I'm sure that's . . . very nice . . ."

"All my friends go away," said Ratpunzel sadly.

"I have lots of them, but Mother Gothel doesn't like them. She always forgives me, though."

"We'll come back," said Wilbur.

"But you probably shouldn't tell Mother Gothel that we were here," added Harriet hurriedly. "Wilbur's . . . uh . . . the son of one of her friends, and . . ."

"It's a surprise!" said Wilbur.

A SURPRISE? SHOULD I BAKE A CAKE?

"Yes!" said Harriet. "A cake would be perfect! A big one! But don't tell her what it's for, or that we're here, or it'll ruin the surprise!"

"Wonderful!" Ratpunzel began to root through the cookbooks. "Oh, I have a great recipe and I'm almost sure I know what went wrong last time!"

She paused, her arms full of books. "But you'll come back? You promise? Mother Gothel leaves for days at a time to get supplies, and I have no one to cook for but me."

"Oh, yes," said Harriet. "Just try to stop us. But we should probably be going now."

"Yes," said Wilbur. He was starting to look a bit overwhelmed. "Yes."

"We'll come back tomorrow," said Harriet.

"That sounds lovely," said Ratpunzel. "We can have tea, and I'll show you my plans for the cake!"

She lowered them back down on her tail and

waved from the window as they walked away.

When they were out of earshot, Wilbur sagged a little and said, "So the prince is stuck in a tree. How is she doing it?"

Harriet shrugged. "I'm not a witch! For all I know, turning people into trees is . . . like . . . super-basic evil witchcraft!"

"Is there someone we could ask?"

LOTS OF PEOPLE. BUT I DON'T THINK WE CAN GET TO ANY OF THEM BEFORE THE EGG HATCHES.

"I'm more interested in Ratpunzel," said Harriet. "She's a bit odd, isn't she?"

"I think she's sweet," said Wilbur. "She's been stuck in a tower her whole life. You have to make allowances."

"Mmm," said Harriet. "You'd think she'd figure out that there's something weird going on."

"Not everybody is as suspicious as you are," said Wilbur. "Anyway, maybe in her world it's normal for people to leave and then a carving to show up. She probably thinks that everybody does that."

Harriet snorted. "You might be right."

"But what are we going to *do?*" asked Wilbur. "Even if we took the egg—we can't just leave Ratpunzel there!"

"No," said Harriet. She squared her shoulders. "No, we can't." She'd rescued plenty of princesses. A few of them had even been glad to see her. The others had just been grumpy that she wasn't a handsome prince. "We'll just have to find another way."

CHAPTER 9

The next morning, they got up early and went back to the clearing.

"Ratpunzel!" called Harriet from the foot of the tower. "Psst!"

She appeared in the window. "Hello! It's all right, she's not back yet."

A moment later, she had hooked her tail over the bar and dropped it down the side of the tower.

"It really doesn't hurt when you do that?" asked Harriet, once she reached the top.

"Nope!"

Wilbur was puffing by the time they pulled him up. "If I keep doing that, I'll need to get in much better shape . . ."

Harriet slapped him on the back. "Have a seat. Ratpunzel, would you mind if I . . . uh . . . made some tea?"

"No," said Ratpunzel. "Go ahead." She smiled.

She was very sweet and very eager to please. Harriet almost felt guilty about the fact that she was taking advantage of Ratpunzel's good nature.

Almost.

Gothel started it by stealing Heady's egg. We're just stealing it back. And we're going to rescue Ratpunzel too.

She left Wilbur and Ratpunzel talking and hurried down the stairs. She could hear their voices from behind her, echoing down the stairwell.

"So what is your day like?" asked Wilbur.

"Oh, not nearly so exciting as yours, I imagine," said Ratpunzel. "I wake up and make breakfast for myself. If Mother Gothel is home, I make breakfast for her. And then I do a few laps of the tower, and practice cartwheels. I can do a no-handed cartwheel!"

Harriet was vaguely envious. She could never manage a no-handed cartwheel. Gravity was not kind to solidly built hamsters.

"And then I read up on the history of cooking for a little while, and then it's time to make lunch . . ."

Harriet reached the kitchen.

She filled the teakettle and set it on the stove to heat, then made her way toward Gothel's bedroom door.

It was locked.

This would stop many princesses, but Harriet was a special breed.

NORMALLY I'D JUST KICK THE DOOR DOWN, BUT I SUPPOSE THAT'D BE RUDE . . .

"And then I read cookbooks some more . . ."

"That's . . . a lot of cooking . . ." said Wilbur.

Harriet pulled a piece of metal out of the lining of her sleeve. (She had taken to keeping one there after she had been arrested and thrown in a dungeon, on charges that she had been almost *completely* innocent of, except for the bit with the chicken.)

"That chicken needed smacking, Your Honor," she muttered. "And the pastrami sandwich was all I had to smack it with. No jury in the world would have convicted me."

It was a very simple lock. Well, Gothel had only Ratpunzel to worry about—no point in putting a massive padlock on everything.

"And then it's time to make dinner. I've read all my cookbooks cover to cover, of course, but sometimes Mother Gothel brings me new ones. Though I can't always get the herbs. I've never *seen* cilantro."

Harriet slipped into the witch's bedroom.

The tower was clearly tapering as it went up, so each room was smaller than the one beneath. Despite sharing this floor with the kitchen, Gothel's bedroom was enormous. She had a four-poster bed with curtains around it and a wardrobe large enough to store the clothes for an entire legion of gerbils.

"And then Mother Gothel goes to bed and I read for a while. Unless it's Sad Story Time, of course."

"Sad Story Time?" asked Wilbur.

Harriet was barely listening.

She'd found Heady's egg.

It was just as large as she remembered. Gothel had set it carefully in the corner. When Harriet touched the surface, the shell was hard, but warm.

"Reptile eggs get hard before they hatch," she

muttered. "Hydras are reptiles, aren't they? More or less . . ."

She tapped on the egg with a claw and listened.

There was no answering tap. Harriet sagged with relief.

If the baby hydra had been preparing to hatch, it would have tapped on the shell. Snakes and lizards and alligators always tapped. They had to chip their way out of the egg with a special tooth.

STILL HAVE A LITTLE TIME, THEN. THANK GOODNESS. I DON'T KNOW HOW TO TAKE CARE OF A BABY HYDRA.

"And then I cry, of course," Ratpunzel was saying matter-of-factly. "The one about the lost orphans in the woods always makes me cry. Then we harvest the tears and then I get a happy story. How do *you* do Sad Story Time?"

Harriet, who had been only half listening, came suddenly alert.

Sad Story Time? Harvest the tears? What?

"We, uh, don't have Sad Story Time," said Wilbur worriedly.

"You don't? But how do you get the tears?"

"Uh . . . we don't . . ."

"But doesn't everybody save their tears?"

"I don't," said Wilbur, sounding very confused. "I just wipe them away."

Ask the question, Wilbur! Harriet wanted to yell. *Ask her why Gothel harvests the tears!*

"But Mother Gothel says that tears are precious! It'd be like wiping diamonds on your sleeve. And you have to save them because what if you ran out of tears?"

"That's an . . . interesting . . . way of looking at it . . ." said Wilbur.

There was something strange and witchy at work here. Harriet's whiskers were tingling. She turned toward the door, ready to go up and ask more questions about the tears, but then she heard the one sound she had been dreading most in the world.

"Ratpunzel! Ratpunzel! Let down your tail!"

Mother Gothel was back.

CHAPTER 10

Oh no!" Ratpunzel said. "If she finds you here, it'll ruin the surprise! Hide!"

There were scurrying sounds from upstairs.

Harriet took a step toward the door. There hadn't been anyplace in the kitchen to hide, but if she could get up the steps . . .

"Ratpunzel! Where are you?"

"Coming, Mother Gothel! I'm sorry, I was in the bathroom . . ."

No time!

Harriet shut the door, muffling the sounds from overhead, and locked it. It wouldn't do for Gothel to discover that someone had been snooping.

Now, for someplace to hide . . .

She threw open the wardrobe.

". . . um," said Harriet.

Gothel didn't keep clothes in the wardrobe.

Instead, both doors were covered in tiny stoppered vials. Each one had a neat, handwritten label on it, with a date. They were full of clear liquid.

TEARS – AUGUST 29TH,
YEAR OF THE CROAKING FROG

"This has taken an unexpected turn," muttered Harriet.

Directly in front of her, inside the wardrobe itself, were a small table, a pair of gloves, and a book.

The book was open. Harriet scanned the words frantically.

Being an Infallible Potion to Trap One's Enemies in the Hearts of Trees read the title.

"I'm glad you're back, Mother Gothel!" said Ratpunzel, directly overhead. Her voice was loud enough to be a warning.

To open the tree, place three drops of the essence upon a knife blade and slice open the bark. Thrust your enemy within the hole, then throw the essence upon them, and the bark shall close again. The tree shall hold them fast, and none shall be freed, even unto the end of the world, except by the essence itself.

A recipe followed.

Harriet palmed a vial of the liquid—you never knew what might come in handy—and shut the wardrobe.

Footsteps came down the stairwell. Harriet looked around wildly for another place to hide.

She dove under the bed.

It was dusty under there, and she had an immediate desire to sneeze. She watched the door from under the bedskirt and tried to breathe through her mouth.

There was a rattling at the door as Mother Gothel unlocked it, and then it opened. "I'm going to bed," said Gothel over her shoulder. "It was a long walk. I can't believe we ran out of flour."

"I made sugar-and-shrimp pancakes while you were gone," said Ratpunzel. "Several times."

"Make fewer pancakes!" She slammed the door.

Harriet's nose was really starting to itch now.

The elderly gerbil dropped a pack by the door and went to the egg.

Harriet raised her eyebrows.

"You'll be so beautiful," crooned Gothel. "So many heads! And you'll guard the tower so well, and you'll be able to cook. That idiot hamster I knew in college went on and on about how well your mother cooks. I'm so tired of Ratpunzel. She can't follow a recipe to save her life. She keeps trying to add trout flakes and squid ink. You wouldn't believe it."

Please, thought Harriet. *Please don't tell me that Gothel kidnapped Heady's egg so that she could get a better cook!*

Harriet was used to villains having very weird motivations, but there were limits. She'd once had to fight off a dragon who was kidnapping people because it wanted their hats. It didn't realize that the hats came off, so it had amassed quite a collection over the years, both of hats and disgruntled prisoners.

This was, if anything, worse.

"You'll guard the castle," Gothel told the egg, "and we won't have any more of these foolish princes coming along to make googly eyes at Ratpunzel. I am getting so tired of dealing with princes."

Aren't we all? thought Harriet. *But we don't go sticking them in trees!*

"You'd think they'd stay away from a tower in the middle of nowhere! How do they even find the place? It's like there's signs up saying 'Hey, magical maiden held in a tower, this way!'"

(Harriet actually had noticed this phenomenon. If you wanted to hide something, the worst possible place you could put it was an isolated fortress in the middle of nowhere surrounded by monsters. Heroes would drop out of the sky to find it. If Harriet had wanted to hide something, she would have gone to a busy marketplace in the middle of the day and just thrown a tablecloth over it.)

"There are so many things I could be doing with her tears!" said Gothel, rapping on the egg with her knuckles. "You don't even know!"

Well, obviously it doesn't know. It's an egg.

"It's the whole reason I kidnapped her," Gothel informed the egg. "I just thought she'd be a better cook."

Harriet rolled her eyes under the bed.

THE TEARS OF A MAGICAL MAIDEN TRUE AND FAIR . . . SUCH MAGIC! AND I VERY NEARLY HAVE A POTION OF IMMORTALITY WORKED OUT! WE'LL LIVE FOR A THOUSAND YEARS, YOU AND I, LITTLE HYDRA!

Gothel paused. ". . . well. And I suppose Rat-punzel too. We'll need to keep the source of the tears around. Maybe we can keep her in the basement or something."

Yikes! thought Harriet. *Bad enough to keep her in a tower all her life, but then to exile her to a basement?*

She must have made some small, stifled sound, because Gothel looked up suspiciously.

WHAT'S THAT? IS SOMEONE THERE? RATPUNZEL, IS THAT YOU?

She pushed away from the egg, looking around the room. Harriet tensed.

I'll jump out. I'll charge her. I'll knock her over before she knows what's happening. I hope she can't do anything witchy on short notice. Bark is not my color!

Gothel moved toward the bed.

And then, from the next room, came an ear-splitting shriek.

CHAPTER 11

It was the teakettle.

Gothel groaned and changed direction. She flung open the door. "Rat*punzel*!"

"Sorry!" cried Ratpunzel from upstairs. "I'll get it—just a minute—I have to finish picking up my tail—"

The teakettle continued to shriek.

SHRIEK!!

Gothel stalked into the kitchen. "Stupid girl! How long does it take to pick up your tail?"

"It's a very long tail, Mother Gothel . . ."

SHRIIIEEEEK! went the teakettle.

Harriet saw her chance.

She lunged out from under the bed and scurried to the door.

Mother Gothel had her back to Harriet and was rummaging through the drawers. The kettle wailed like a hungry ghost.

One chance . . . thought Harriet, and tiptoed for the stairs.

Harriet went up the stairs and met Ratpunzel coming down. They exchanged wide-eyed looks.

"Ratpunzel!" screamed Gothel. "There are no potholders in this kitchen!"

"I usually use my tail, Mother Gothel . . ." She hurried down the steps with her tail curling and wriggling behind her.

Harriet made it up the stairs, walking as lightly as she could. With all the racket, Gothel *probably* couldn't hear her footsteps, but she would have hated to be wrong.

When she reached the top, she looked around wildly. "Psst! Wilbur? Are you here?"

"Up here!" whispered Wilbur.

Harriet hurried up the ladder to Ratpunzel's sleeping loft. She didn't see Wilbur.

"Wilbur?"

"You're under the pile of cookbooks?" she whispered.

"Yes, the corners are awfully pointy! And I think I just learned a new way to slice avocados!"

Harriet hunkered down behind the pile.

The teakettle stopped.

"You can't just turn the kettle on and forget it, stupid girl!" Gothel growled. "You'll burn the tower down!"

"Sorry, Mother Gothel . . ."

"Oh yeah," whispered Harriet, to herself as much as to Wilbur. "We're getting her out of here."

They heard Gothel stomp across the floor and slam the door. A few minutes later, Ratpunzel came up the ladder. "Stay quiet," she whispered. "She'll be asleep soon."

"How will we know?" whispered Wilbur, some-what muffled by cookbooks.

SHE SNORES REALLY LOUD.

And indeed, after a few minutes a noise began to drift up the stairs that sounded vaguely like a goose being squashed in an accordion.

Ratpunzel beckoned them down the ladder.

Wilbur emerged from his hiding place, shedding cookbooks.

In silence, Ratpunzel draped her tail over the bar on the window.

She and Wilbur climbed down. The tip of Ratpunzel's tail waved to them as they hurried away into the forest.

CHAPTER 12

Okay," said Harriet. She began ticking things off on her fingers. "We need to get Ratpunzel out."

"Yes," said Wilbur.

"Qwerk," said Mumfrey.

"Qwerrrk," said Hyacinth.

"And we need to get Heady's egg out of the tower."

"Definitely."

"Qwerk."

"Qwerrrk."

"And we need to get both the egg and Ratpunzel to someplace safe."

"Right."

"Qwerk."

"Qwerrrk."

Harriet looked around the circle of faces, two quail, one hamster, all watching her expectantly.

"So . . . anybody got any ideas?"

Harriet sighed.

"Well, I can figure out the first one," she said. "And maybe even the second one. And then . . . um . . . we'll improvise, I guess."

She twiddled her fingers a bit.

"The biggest problem," she said finally, "is getting into the tower."

"Well, that's not hard," said Wilbur. "You go up and ask Ratpunzel to let you in."

Harriet shook her head. "No, I mean getting into the tower another way. We're super-vulnerable climbing up and down, and I can't possibly carry that egg myself."

"But you heard Ratpunzel," said Wilbur. "There's no other way in."

"That's your problem, Wilbur," said Harriet. "You're so *trusting*. And so's Ratpunzel. I mean, it's sweet, don't get me wrong, but seriously."

Wilbur blinked.

"Look, think about it," said Harriet. "You build a tower, right? And then you want to put a stove and a bed and a bunch of other stuff in it. How are you gonna do that if there's no way up?"

"Errr . . . ladders?" asked Wilbur.

"You ever tried to carry a stove up a ladder? And even then, how would you fit it through the window?"

Wilbur was silent for a minute. The quails shuffled their feet.

OKAY, WHEN YOU PUT IT LIKE THAT, IT DOES SOUND SORT OF IMPROBABLE . . .

"And Gothel's not stupid," said Harriet. "Suppose Ratpunzel falls out the window? Or just refuses to throw down her tail one day? How is she gonna get back inside?"

"She could . . . uh . . . hmm . . ."

"Unless she can fly, she has to have another way into the tower. I mean, a tower with no doors *sounds* cool, but I'll bet you a nickel that there's another way in."

She drummed her fingers on her quail's saddle. "I can get us in," she said. "I think. Probably. But I'm gonna need a few things . . ."

"Why does this always end up with you handing me a shopping list?" asked Wilbur a few minutes later.

"Oh, *one* other time," said Harriet. "And that ended great! All those cans of paint in the mouse kingdom . . . ha! That was awesome."

Wilbur looked at the list glumly. "Are you sure you need all this stuff?"

"Yep."

"The ax?"

"The ax is critical."

"The chalk?"

"The chalk is *super*-critical."

"The bungee cords?"

"Bungee cords are the single most useful object in the universe, Wilbur. People may say it's duct tape, but it's actually bungee cords. All great heroes know this."

HERCULES? ACHILLES? CONAN THE VETERINARIAN? THEY ALL KNEW THE VALUE OF BUNGEE CORDS. TRUE STORY.

Wilbur shook his head and climbed onto Hyacinth's back. They trotted away into the Forest of Misery.

Harriet rubbed Mumfrey's feathers. Her quail made a happy "Qwerk!" noise.

JUST BETWEEN YOU AND ME, MUMFREY, I'M A LITTLE WORRIED ABOUT THIS ONE.

"I mean," said Harriet, "I can get *into* the tower. There's always a way in. Sure, sometimes you need to use a sledgehammer, but you can still get in. And I can get the egg out, and getting Ratpunzel out is easy. But then we're going to be saddled with three people and a really heavy egg, and only two quails."

"Qwerk!" said Mumfrey.

"I know *you* can carry two riders," said Harriet. "Or one rider and an egg. But Hyacinth can't carry two. She's not a battle quail. Did you see how fast she shlopped, though? Like a regular racing quail! If we put Ratpunzel on her, no way will Gothel be able to catch her."

She scratched Mumfrey's topknot.

AND THAT MEANS THAT WHEN GOTHEL COMES FOR US, ONE OF US IS GOING TO HAVE TO STAY BEHIND . . .

Harriet knew perfectly well who that ought to be. She was Harriet the Formerly Invincible! She had fought the Fairy Ratshade and the Witch Molezelda! She had beaten Ogrecats and collapsed the mouse king's castle!

As heroes went, Harriet was a pretty big deal. She was very nearly famous. It was probably only a matter of time before someone showed up to license Harriet-branded adventuring equipment.

The problem, as she would be the first to tell you, was that the bigger you are . . . the harder you fall.

CHAPTER 13

The sun was setting when Wilbur returned from the Kingdom of Sunshine, carrying a heavy sack of equipment. He handed it over, along with the change.

"They were very nice at the hardware store," said Wilbur.

Harriet sniffed. She did not trust hardware stores where people were nice. The ideal hardware store, as far as she was concerned, had one ancient, surly rodent in the back who glared at you when you asked for anything. All the screws and rivets and washers were in tiny unmarked drawers or shoved in paper sacks thrown in a pile in the corner. The ancient rodent knew where everything was, and you had to ask and get glared at.

If you could find anything on your own, they weren't doing it right.

Wilbur, who liked things to be clearly marked and didn't feel the need to earn the respect of ancient surly hardware store owners, did not agree.

Nevertheless, he'd done a good job. She had everything she'd asked for.

"Could you not wave that ax around?" asked Wilbur. "It makes me nervous."

"I'm a professional," said Harriet. "I took an Ax Safety Class."

Wilbur stared at her.

SERIOUSLY?

I GOT PERFECT GRADES IN BRANDISHING.

"You got . . . graded . . . on . . . brandishing."

"Well, you wouldn't want to wave an ax just *any* old way. Somebody might get hurt."

SOMETIMES YOU WORRY ME . . .

As soon as darkness fell, they crept toward the tower. Harriet led them in a wide circle, out of view of the window. Unfortunately, that meant that a sea of thorns stood between the heroes and the tower.

"Stay here, Mumfrey," she said. "You too, Hyacinth. When we yell, come running."

"Qwerk."

Under cover of darkness, Wilbur and Harriet approached the wall of thorns.

"We don't have to hack our way through this one, do we?" asked Wilbur. "Because I've still got blisters from that one time."

"Nah," said Harriet. "Minimal hacking. Hacking Light. A few moments of hacking at most."

Wilbur sighed.

Harriet selected a spot just to one side of the tower window. If Gothel had leaned out and

looked down, she might have been able to see the hamsters, but there was no help for it. Hopefully she was sound asleep.

The thorns were dense here, but thinned rapidly toward the base of the tower. Harriet was betting that if there was a door, it was in the clear spot under the window. You'd hate to use your escape route only to find yourself surrounded by impassable vegetation.

She pulled the ax off her shoulder and started chopping.

WHACK! WHACK! WHACK!

"It's just like old times!" she said happily.

"I can already feel the blisters . . ." said Wilbur gloomily.

Despite Wilbur's fears, it only took them a few minutes to chop a passage through the thorns. Many of the plants were dry and split apart at a single blow of the ax. Harriet hummed as she worked, then began to sing under her breath.

"Oh, if I had an ax, I'd chop all over this land . . ."

"Don't sing," said Wilbur, putting his hands over his ears. "You're a great fighter and a pretty good princess and you're one of the smartest people I know, but you really, *really* cannot sing."

Harriet laughed. It was nice of Wilbur to say that she was smart. She didn't mind that she couldn't sing. She didn't want to be an opera singer anyway. Opera singers hardly ever got to slay dragons.

When she reached the tower wall, she turned sideways and began chopping a path around the edge. The moonlight on the thorns cast sharp-edged shadows over the ground.

Wilbur took over and hacked through the last few yards. Harriet glanced up nervously.

The open window looked like an empty eye socket.

Just don't anybody come and look down . . .

"Now, then," said Harriet, "it's chalk time . . ."
She fished out the pack of chalk.

Wilbur put his chin in his hand. "I'm still wondering how you're going to open a door with chalk."

"Watch and learn," said Harriet, and began to scribble on the side of the tower.

CHAPTER 14

The tower was gray. The chalk was white. The stones were smooth and fit together with hardly any cracks, and as far as Harriet was concerned, that was perfect.

She used the side of the stick of chalk and ran it over the stone, leaving long white stripes.

At first, she saw nothing. Just white stripes on gray rocks. Wilbur looked unimpressed.

She worked her way across the front of the tower, starting to get worried. If what she was looking for wasn't here, she was going to have to chop her way through the rest of the thorns.

Her heart had just started to sink, and then the chalk suddenly revealed a thin, bright white line.

Harriet had a strong urge to cheer. *Yes!*

She worked the chalk vigorously along the line. The fine white dust filled up the narrow crack. It practically glowed in the moonlight.

"There," said Harriet, stepping back. "That's the door."

The crack formed the outline of a square doorway. It would have been completely invisible if not for the chalk.

Wilbur let out a low whistle. "Okay," he admitted. "That's pretty cool. How did you guess?"

"There's a secret passage in my mom and dad's castle," said Harriet. "Only Dad is really absentminded and he keeps forgetting where it is." She dropped the chalk back in the bag. "So about twice a year we have to go over the wall in his study with chalk and find it again."

"So you've found it," said Wilbur. "But how do we open it?"

Harriet ran her hands over the door. "Good question. It has to open from this side, because otherwise she couldn't get back into the tower . . ."

Wilbur and Harriet took turns poking the stones. There were chips and fine cracks in the surface, but nothing that resembled a doorknob. If it hadn't been for the chalk outline, there would have been nothing at all to indicate a door there.

Eventually Harriet gave up in disgust. She leaned against the wall, sighing. "So close . . ."

She rubbed her shoulder, which was a little sore from swinging the ax around. An unfamiliar weight in the sleeve surprised her.

OH, HUH. FORGOT ABOUT THIS . . .

The vial glittered in the moonlight. Harriet read the label again. "Tears—August 29th, Year of the Croaking Frog."

"What's that?" asked Wilbur.

"I think it's Ratpunzel's tears," said Harriet slowly. "Gothel was going on and on about the tears of a maiden pure and fair. I guess that's Ratpunzel."

"It's sure not you . . ." muttered Wilbur.

"Hey! I'm always fair! Mostly!"

"I don't know if you're purely *anything*, though. Except maybe pure Harriet."

Harriet considered this. There were much worse things to be than purely yourself. She tucked the vial back in her jacket. "Well, anyway, I don't see how tears will help us much. Gothel said she can do magic with them, but that's not getting this door open." She scowled at the side of the tower. "And anyway, she said it to the egg."

"Do you think she was telling the truth?" asked Wilbur.

"Who'd lie to an egg?"

In the end, it was Wilbur who figured it out.

One of the chips in the stone concealed a latch. He dug his fingers down into it and heard a click.

The stone door swung open.

"You're the best, Wilbur," said Harriet.

There was a narrow open space, just large enough for the door to swing inward, and beyond it, a spiral staircase leading up into darkness.

Harriet put a finger to her lips. The stone walls might muffle the sounds while they were outside, but they would probably bounce an echo upward and directly to the sleeping Gothel.

"Come on," she whispered to Wilbur. "Let's go find that egg."

CHAPTER 15

The two hamsters crept up the spiral staircase. It was dusty inside. Judging by the lack of footprints, no one had come this way for some time.

Harriet glanced back behind them and saw their tracks marking each step.

Well, it wasn't like Gothel wouldn't have been able to figure out that *somebody'd* been in the tower . . .

"What do we do when we get there?" whispered Wilbur as they climbed. "Should I get Ratpunzel?"

"Not yet," said Harriet. "You gotta strap the egg to my back first. I'm pretty sure I can carry it, but I'll fall down the stairs if I'm holding it in my arms."

"How are we going to get Gothel out of her bedroom?"

Harriet sighed. "We just have to hope she's a sound sleeper."

"What if she's a light sleeper?!"

They reached the top of the stairs.

There was a door there, cut to follow the shape of the stones. Harriet reached for the doorknob.

The door swung open. Harriet kept a paw on the doorknob, ready to stop it in case the hinges squeaked.

But they did not squeak. Slowly, an inch at a time, she eased her way silently into the room.

She had been hoping to come out in the kitchen, or at the base of the other staircase.

Of course, if you want a secret way in and out of the tower, you'd want it to be where you could get to it easily, if something went wrong . . .

Harriet had stepped into Gothel's bedroom.

She looked at the bed, ready to jump backward.

She didn't need to worry. Gothel wasn't there.

The blankets were smooth. Wherever Gothel was, she hadn't gone to bed yet.

Harriet was trying to figure out what to do next when she heard the witch's voice echoing from overhead.

"And then the sad little mouse saw the baby quail that she loved more than anything in the world get eaten by horrible weasel-wolves!"

"Oh no!" cried Ratpunzel. "Oh, poor quail! Was there blood?"

"Lots," said Gothel. "Also guts. It was dreadful."

"Nooooo . . ."

Wilbur came through the doorway and saw the egg. His face lit up and he ran to it. Harriet put a finger to her lips and pointed up at the ceiling, in the direction of the voices.

". . . so now the sad little mouse was all alone, with nobody to love her. Her parents had been killed by bandits and her brother had fallen into a pit full of spikes and her best friend died of extreme sunburn and her baby quail was eaten by weasel-wolves, and so the sad little mouse went sadly back home . . .

". . . but when she got home, she found that the house had been struck by lightning and it was on fire . . ."

"Oh, sad mouse, no!"

". . . and no matter how much she cried, her tears couldn't put out the flames."

"That is *messed up*," said Harriet.

"It's Sad Story Time," said Wilbur. "Just like Rat-punzel said."

"It's *Stupid* Story Time," muttered Harriet. "You can't put out a fire by crying on it. Form a bucket brigade. And why didn't she fight off the weasel-wolves?"

She went over to the egg. It was brilliantly white, even in the dimness of the bedroom. "Okay. Let's get this thing on my back while she's distracted."

Wilbur patted the shell absently. "It's okay, little egg. We'll get you home . . ."

It tapped at him.

Harriet blinked.

She poked the shell with her nail, making a tiny *tick!* noise.

Tap! Tap! came from inside the shell.

"Uh-oh," said Wilbur.

". . . so then the sad little mouse's house had burned down and all her toys were charred to ashes . . ."

"Nooo!"

Harriet gritted her teeth, but it was Wilbur who said it out loud.

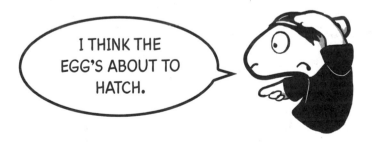

I THINK THE EGG'S ABOUT TO HATCH.

CHAPTER 16

They stared at the egg. From overhead, Gothel was embarking on the next of the sad little mouse's travails, where a kind hedgehog took her in and then promptly came down with fatal hedge pox.

"What do you think?" asked Wilbur.

"I think anybody that racks up a body count like that is probably secretly murdering them herself. I mean, how *did* her brother fall into the pit of spikes?"

Wilbur stared at her. "About the *egg*," he said.

"Oh, right." Harriet frowned down at the egg.

"I guess all we can do is try to get it out of here and hope that it doesn't hatch while I'm carrying it. . . ."

She pulled out the bungee cords and looped them over her waist, harness-style. "Let's do this."

Wilbur set to work.

The egg was heavy. *Really* heavy. Harriet was sure now that Gothel had been using magic to carry it. Harriet had been swinging a sword for years and had the muscles to prove it, and the egg still threatened to flatten her.

"And then the kind hedgehog's burrow collapsed, trapping the sad little mouse's foot in the rubble. She cried and cried, because she was all alone in the world and her foot hurt and . . ."

They could hear Ratpunzel sniffling overhead.

Wilbur got the last of the bungee cords arranged and said, "Okay . . . try to stand up . . ."

Harriet staggered to her feet.

"Ooof . . ."

She had to lean far forward to keep the egg from pulling her over backward. She could feel the baby hydra inside tapping, somewhere in the vicinity of her rib cage.

Harriet made it to the hidden staircase and started down.

"I think that's enough for Sad Story Time tonight," said Gothel.

"But what about the poor mouse? Her foot was stuck!" said Ratpunzel. Her voice sounded all fluttery, as if she was crying.

"Oh, right," said Gothel. "Um, she was eaten by more weasel-wolves."

"The same ones who—*sob*—ate her baby quail?"

"Yeah, sure," said Gothel. "Have a nice night!"

"Go faster!" whispered Wilbur. "I think she's done!"

"I can't go any faster!" snapped Harriet. "I'm carrying a great big honking egg on my back! If I go any faster, I'm going to get squashed sunnyside up!"

"Then what do we do?"

"Hide under the bed! When she goes to sleep, go get Ratpunzel out! I'll take care of the egg!"

"Got it!" Wilbur scurried back up the stairs. Harriet heard the soft click of the door closing.

It was almost a good plan.

Harriet got another three steps down and thought, *Wait a minute—she's going to notice the egg is missing, isn't she?*

The problem with improvising rescue plans is that in the heat of the moment, you can overlook very important things.

She paused on the stairs, teetering back and forth. The baby hydra tapped her again.

I could go put the egg back and wait and . . . No, that's stupid . . . uh . . . uh . . . Okay, I could go put a fake egg back . . . Can I make a fake egg out of bungee cords?

And then she heard the bedroom door open and a scream of fury echoed down the stairs.

"Where is my egg?!"

Harriet began to run.

CHAPTER 17

Running down stairs with a giant egg tied to your back is a nerve-racking experience. Harriet bounced off the walls like a pinball, swinging the egg to avoid striking it on the stones. There was just enough slack to the cords that when she hit a wall, the egg would slam into her back.

The baby hydra began hammering on her ribs. She hoped it wasn't scared.

"It'll be okay!" she told the egg. "I promise! I think!"

Overhead, the door to the stairs slammed open.

She lumbered down the stairs, trying desperately to protect the egg.

"I'll use your guts for fertilizer!" screamed Gothel.

Harriet could hear footsteps on the stairs as Gothel chased her.

The gerbil was a lot faster, given that she wasn't carrying a massive egg on her back. On the other hand, Harriet had a head start.

This is the worst race ever, she thought, bouncing off another wall. Her shoulder was going to be black-and-blue tomorrow.

"Who are you?" Gothel shouted. "Where did you come from?"

It occurred to Harriet that as soon as Gothel got a good look at her, she'd realize Harriet was the same hamster she'd met on the road . . . and would realize that Wilbur had to be around somewhere as well.

I have to keep her distracted! Uh—uh—"I'm an egg collector!" shouted Harriet. "I saw you carrying yours and decided to steal it! By myself!"

Gothel sounded much closer than Harriet was comfortable with.

"How did you get in? Did that idiot Ratpunzel let you in?"

"Don't know what you're talking about!"

She staggered around the final turn and saw the open doorway. Moonlight streamed in and cast a long white arc across the floor.

Harriet leaped through the door, spun around, and slammed it shut.

Gothel hit the door a moment later.

"Open this door at once!" shouted Gothel, hammering on it.

"Oh, sure," said Harriet. "I am absolutely going to open the door that I am holding closed, just because you ordered me to. *Why* does anyone ever think that will work?"

There was a brief pause from the other side of the door. "That's not a bad question," Gothel admitted.

"I know, right?"

The gerbil smacked the door again. Harriet leaned against it. The weight of the egg helped pin the door closed.

"*Please* open this door?"

"Sorry," said Harriet. "I appreciate that you said please, but no."

"Then it appears we are at an impasse," said Gothel.

Harriet, who had always quite liked the word *impasse*, wished that she'd been the one to say that.

Something odd was happening to the egg. Harriet turned her head and saw a tiny chip of eggshell fall away.

Her first thought was that she had broken the egg in her headlong flight down the steps.

Her second thought was that the egg was hatching right now, this minute, and this was going to be a real problem.

Her third thought was "Ow!" because at that moment, Ratpunzel's tail fell from the sky and hit her across the face.

CHAPTER 18

Wilbur came sliding down the tail and landed next to Harriet. "What's happening? Where's Gothel?"

"How do you know my name?" yelled Gothel through the door. "And why does your voice sound familiar?"

"Oh, I see," said Wilbur.

"Hey!" Gothel sounded surprised. "I know that voice! You're Hazel's boy! And that must be your fat little hamster friend!"

"That was uncalled for," said Harriet. "I am sturdy, I'll have you know. This is pure muscle."

"I am going to write your mother a very stern letter!"

Wilbur winced.

Harriet looked up. Ratpunzel was doing something complicated with her tail and the bar outside the window. "Are you ready?" she called.

"Ready!" said Wilbur.

"Ratpunzel?" demanded Gothel. "What are you doing? Stay away from this egg thief!"

Ratpunzel came sliding down her own tail. Wilbur held out his arms and caught the young rat as she landed.

Ratpunzel hopped down. Her tail was still hanging in the air. She gave a hard yank, and suddenly it was falling around them in long pink loops.

"How'd you do that?" asked Harriet.

"Slipknot," said Ratpunzel. She stood on tiptoes and touched the egg. "Oh! There's a wee little snaky face in there!"

"You better not be hurting that egg!" shouted Gothel.

"We're trying not to!" Harriet looked around. "Somebody find me something to brace this door with, will you? Other than myself?"

"Mother Gothel!" said Ratpunzel. "What are you doing there?"

"You know that the world is full of monsters! They're going to eat you!"

Ratpunzel looked at Harriet.

I'VE NEVER EATEN ANYONE! EXCEPT THAT ONE TIME, AND HE SHOULDN'T HAVE BEEN SLEEPING IN THE CASSEROLE DISH!

AND YOU'RE THE MONSTER! NOBODY OUT HERE TELLS PEOPLE SAD STORIES TO MAKE THEM CRY JUST SO THEY CAN GET TEARS OUT OF THEM!

THEY DON'T?

Wilbur found the ax and began trying to jam the blade into the doorframe to wedge it shut.

The egg trembled. Another chip fell out.

"You told me there wasn't a door!" said Ratpunzel.

". . . uh," said Gothel. "Ah. The door. Um. I can explain?"

"So explain!"

". . . give me a minute."

"I can't believe you lied about the door!" shouted Ratpunzel. "I could have gone out with you!"

"Monsters," said Gothel. "Lots of monsters!"

"They never ate *you!* I was going to bake you a cake!" cried Ratpunzel. "A cake with sprinkles and three kinds of filling and smoked salmon on top!"

"I think that'll hold," said Wilbur. "At least for a little bit . . ."

Harriet nodded. She stepped away from the

door, hefted the egg up, and began stumbling toward the woods.

Another chip of eggshell fell.

Gothel apparently realized that the others were leaving and redoubled her attack on the door. The ax handle bounced as she slammed against the door.

Harriet tried to move faster. The egg seemed to get heavier with every step. Her back was killing her.

Wilbur and Ratpunzel caught up easily. "Ah . . . can you move any faster?" asked Wilbur, glancing back at the door. "I don't think that's going to hold her for very long . . ."

"No," said Harriet shortly. "Unless you want to help."

Wilbur got behind her and tried to help lift up the egg.

"This weighs a ton!" gasped Wilbur.

"No kidding!"

They staggered forward.

Harriet could see the trees and Mumfrey waiting. She was starting to think that she might actually make it.

Two loud sounds echoed through the clearing.

The first was the sound of the hydra egg cracking. Something wet oozed down the back of Harriet's neck. It felt nasty.

"It's hatching!" cried Wilbur, alarmed. "I mean—I mean—it's coming out!"

"Hello, little friend!" cooed Ratpunzel.

"It looks just like Heady!" said Wilbur, sounding both terrified and delighted. "Only tiny!"

The second sound was much more ominous.

It was the sound of the ax falling out of the crack in the doorjamb.

The tower door slammed open.

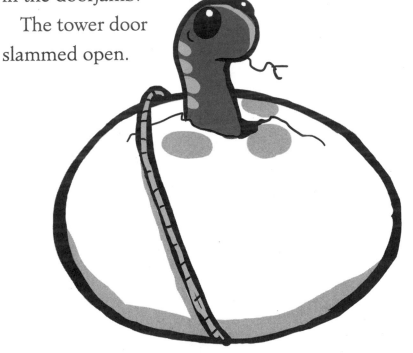

CHAPTER 19

Harriet turned.

Gothel ran toward them. Her ears were flat back and her long tail lashed from side to side like an angry Ogrecat's.

"Right," said Harriet. "Wilbur, get this egg off me."

She shrugged out of the bungee cord harness. Wilbur took the weight of the baby hydra and staggered.

Harriet didn't take her eyes off Gothel. "Move! I'll hold her off!"

"I won't leave you!" said Ratpunzel, who had read a lot of stories about heroic last stands (which, given Sad Story Time, had always ended badly).

"Or you could, y'know, do what she says," said Wilbur, who knew Harriet quite well. A heroic last stand might end badly, but disobeying Harriet's orders would end like the apocalypse, only with more screaming.

"But what if you *die?*" cried Ratpunzel. "Like the sad little mouse—"

THEN I WILL COME BACK AND HAUNT YOU FOR NOT FOLLOWING ORDERS!

Wilbur, with his arms full of shell, said, "Uh, Ratpunzel, can you help me? The hydra's getting squirmy . . ."

"Oh!" She hurried to the hamster's side. "Who's a good little hydra, then?"

Harriet breathed a sigh of relief as Wilbur led Ratpunzel back toward the trees.

Gothel halted, just out of arm's reach. She glared at Harriet and rolled up her sleeves. "Out of my way, hamster! You won't keep that hydra!"

"It belongs with its mother," said Harriet.

"I'll take better care of it!"

"Like you have Ratpunzel?"

I'VE TAKEN EXCELLENT CARE OF RATPUNZEL!

"You lied to her about the outside world! You turned the people who came to see her into trees!"

"Being a tree is completely painless!"

She tried to dart past Harriet.

Harriet had a healthy respect for magic, for people who did magic, and for the strength of unlikely-looking people.

On the other hand, sometimes you really only had one option.

She pounced on Gothel.

They rolled over and over through the clearing. Gothel kicked and bit and snarled, sounding more like a wild animal than a gerbil. Harriet tried to keep from getting her eyes scratched out and hoped that Wilbur was getting the egg and Ratpunzel well away from the clearing.

Gothel whipped her tail around and began trying to choke Harriet with it.

"Urrrghg . . ." said Harriet, somewhat frightened but mostly annoyed. She wished she were still invincible.

There was a small chance that Gothel might actually murder her, and that would be really embarrassing.

She drove her elbow into Gothel's stomach. The gerbil went "Oof!" and relaxed her grip.

Harriet took a step forward, gasping for air. Gothel was still clutching her jacket sleeve.

Something small and brightly colored fell out of the sleeve.

Harriet snatched for it, but Gothel was faster.

"Oh . . ." said Gothel, in a soft, satisfied voice. "Oh, you little fool. I can't believe you were stupid enough to carry this with you . . ."

"Uh," said Harriet. "I . . . uh." At the moment, she couldn't believe it either. She knew Gothel did magic with those vials of tears. Why had she been carrying one around?

Well, it was a bit late to wallow in regret now.

Gothel twisted the top off the vial.

Harriet decided that now would be an excellent time to run away.

CHAPTER 20

Contrary to popular opinion, heroes run away a lot. The ones who don't run away in the face of overwhelming odds don't usually live long enough to be recognized as heroes. When you have been turned into a damp splatter underneath a dragon's foot, nobody says, "Wow, look how brave she was!" Usually they just sigh heavily and go get a mop.

Having spent much of her life being invincible, Harriet hadn't run away to save herself very often, but she frequently retreated from battles that looked like they would be dangerous for Mumfrey. It is very rude to be invincible if you get your friends hurt doing it.

Harriet ran.

She didn't run as fast as she wanted to, because her throat still hurt from where Gothel had tried to throttle her, and her lower back was throbbing from carrying a gigantic hydra egg down a tower.

She was also unpleasantly aware that gerbils run faster than hamsters.

(The ancestors of gerbils come from arid deserts and have long legs for leaping. The ancestors of hamsters also come from deserts, but they prefer to loaf around in burrows. Even at her fastest, Harriet moved at a kind of high-speed waddle. There was a reason she rode Mumfrey everywhere.)

ANCESTRAL
GERBIL
↓

ANCESTRAL
HAMSTER
↓

The trees were very close. Harriet ran for them, hoping to lose Gothel in the forest.

"Harriet!" cried Ratpunzel. "Oh, Harriet, run!"

Harriet gritted her teeth. Ratpunzel was supposed to be running, not yelling and giving away her position!

She looked over her shoulder and, sure enough, Gothel was veering away, going after Ratpunzel instead of her.

"No you don't!" gasped Harriet, and changed course toward Ratpunzel.

The forest loomed up before them. Ratpunzel stood on the edge, wringing her hands.

"Don't just *stand* there!" yelled Harriet. "Do something useful!"

Ratpunzel looked blank.

It's not her fault, thought Harriet grimly. *She's been locked in a tower all her life and nobody's let her do anything except cry and cook. She's really done very well, all things considered.*

Still, she wished they'd broken into a tower with a fair maiden who did martial arts and first aid instead.

Gothel reached the trees.

Actually, she reached one particular tree, the one that Harriet had noticed earlier. It didn't seem to have any creatures trapped in it, but the trunk gaped open like a lipless mouth.

She stopped there, beside it, facing Ratpunzel.

"Give me the hydra," said Gothel, holding out her hand. "Give me the hydra, Ratpunzel, and go back in the tower, and we'll just forget this happened."

Ratpunzel looked over her shoulder at Wilbur

and the quails. Wilbur was frantically trying to strap the baby hydra to Mumfrey's saddle.

"But it's somebody else's baby," quavered Rat-punzel. "Wilbur told me. It belongs to a hydra named Heady."

Gothel scowled. "We'll talk about it inside."

From her angle, Harriet could see Gothel holding the vial behind her back.

"It's a trap!" she yelled, and barreled full tilt into the gerbil.

Ratpunzel squeaked and jumped backward, clutching her tail. Gothel flailed at Harriet, but all of Harriet's energy was devoted to pinning the hand with the vial to the gerbil's side.

"Don't let her break the vial!" she shouted. "Ratpunzel, get out of here!"

Gothel rammed her shoulder into Harriet and drove her back against the tree.

Ratpunzel ran. Not away, as Harriet would have liked, but around the tree trunk, trying to put it between her and Gothel.

Gothel lunged after the rat.

Harriet, still clutching Gothel's wrist, stumbled after her.

The hamster made three steps, got Gothel's shoulder, spun the gerbil around, and was just starting to think that things were looking up . . . when she tripped over Ratpunzel's tail.

Harriet fell down hard. She skinned both knees and the palm of her hand. She had a feeling that would hurt later.

Gothel stood over her and raised the vial.

"Now," said Gothel. "Now, thief, I'm going to deal with you!"

She splashed the tears out in a long liquid arc. Harriet threw her hand over her face.

Something heavy knocked her aside.

Harriet heard a *sploosh!* a *thud!* and a very loud *SNAP!*

"*Nooooo!*" cried Ratpunzel.

The hamster rolled sideways, and looked up.

The open tree trunk had slammed closed.

OH, NO! WILBUR!

CHAPTER 21

Harriet stared at the tree that had swallowed her friend.

It was unmistakably Wilbur. It looked like a perfect wooden carving, down to the individual strands of hair and the nails on his hands and his alarmed expression.

"Blast!" said Gothel. She turned the vial over, but it was empty. "I meant to get you, not him! Now, where's my egg?"

Harriet sat up.

"Wilbur!" she said. "I should never have brought you! You were always too nice to be a warrior!"

She grabbed his bark-covered hand. It was wood, definitely wood, not fur and bone. She was afraid that if she pulled on it too hard, it might snap off.

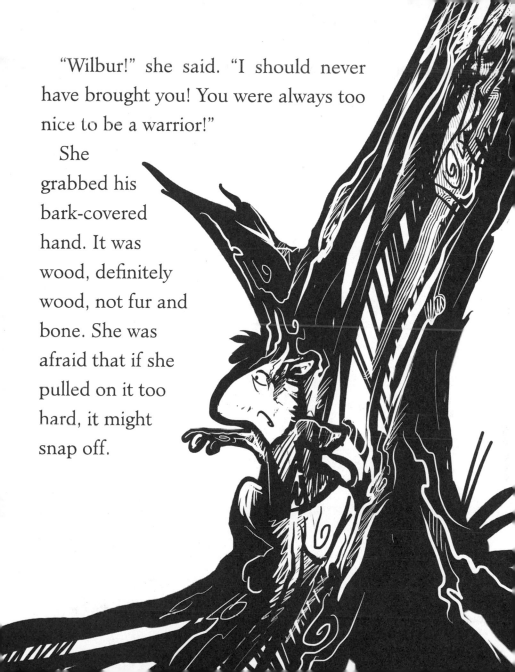

"Don't worry, Wilbur! I'll get you out of there!
Just—err—sit tight—"

"No, you won't," said Gothel. "Not unless you
give me back that egg!"

Harriet looked around. Mumfrey was nowhere
to be seen.

*Thank goodness! At least somebody around here fol-
lows orders!*

ONLY AFTER YOU STOLE IT FIRST! I LIBERATED THAT EGG!

"Well, I'm the only one who knows how to liberate your friend!" shouted Gothel.

Harriet thought fast. If she went after Mumfrey, Gothel would have time to get more tears out of the tower. Who knew what she'd be able to do? She didn't dare leave the gerbil alone with Wilbur—but short of chopping down Wilbur's tree and dragging it with them, what could she do?

"The egg's not here," she said, stalling for time. "I'd have to go and get it back from my quail . . ."

Gothel's whiskers twisted as she scowled. "Then you've got nothing I want, hamster!"

She lifted her hands in front of her. The tips of her claws began to glow.

"What are you doing?" said Harriet.

MAGIC. *OBVIOUSLY.*

"Uh," said Harriet. "I thought you had to work with tears and trees and stuff . . ."

"Mostly," admitted Gothel. "Plants are the only things I can magic up myself. And I don't even like plants very much. They're so *limited*. You've got your wall of thorns and your vine ropes, and then what do you do?"

"Army of giant Venus flytraps?" said Harriet. "Mushrooms with exploding spores that blind your enemies? That's just off the top of my head."

Gothel paused. "Hey, that's pretty good."

Harriet shook her head in disgust. Some people had *no* imagination.

She tried to back away, and discovered that she couldn't. Green bands were snaking up her legs and were holding her in place. She swatted at the plants with her hands, and they whipped out and twined around her wrists.

"I admit," said Gothel, "the vine ropes aren't as impressive as an army of Venus flytraps. I'm going to have to give that some serious thought. But they're good enough for egg thieves!"

"... um," said Harriet.

"You're right, though," said Gothel. "If I want to do *real* magic, I need the tears. Even trapping people in trees is hard. That's why we have Sad Story Time. Pretty soon I'll have enough tears to live forever!"

Harriet rolled her eyes. Villains *always* wanted to live forever. They never seemed to think about how boring it would eventually get.

She tried squirming. It didn't help much. The vines were extremely strong.

"But I'm willing to waste a vial trapping you in a tree," said Gothel. "I'll even put you near your little friend."

She leaned in, very close to Harriet.

Harriet wondered if she was going to be able to gnaw through the vines before Gothel got back from the tower. It didn't seem all that likely.

"Or," said Gothel, sneering, "I *could* just leave you here for the weasel-wolves. I'm sure they'd love the taste of hamster—"

WHACK!

Gothel's expression changed.

It became, very briefly, surprised.

And then she slumped over into the grass, knocked out cold.

Ratpunzel stood over her, clutching the broken half of the hydra eggshell in both hands.

"Was . . . was that useful?" she asked.

Harriet let out a long sigh. "Yeah," she said. "Yeah, it was."

CHAPTER 22

In the end, Ratpunzel had to fetch the ax that they'd used to chop the thorns and then hack the vines loose from around Harriet. Harriet tried not to flinch. Ratpunzel had clearly never taken a class in ax safety.

Still, she'd just brained Gothel with an eggshell, so Harriet was inclined to cut her some slack.

"You did good," she said quietly, shaking the last vines off her arms. "Like, really good." She patted the young rat awkwardly on the shoulder.

Ratpunzel glanced toward Wilbur's tree. "Not good enough," she said.

They used the bungee cords left over from the egg to tie Gothel's hands together.

Hyacinth emerged from the trees. "Qwerk," she said. "Qwerk-erk, qwerk," which is Quail for "Mumfrey's about a mile down the road. Should I get him?"

"Yeah," said Harriet. "Um. Please do that . . ."

She hoped the baby hydra wasn't too frightened.

Hyacinth set off shlopping down the path. She

didn't seem to have noticed that Wilbur was stuck in the tree. Harriet let out a sigh of relief.

Ratpunzel looked at her hopefully. "What do we do now?"

"I'm not sure," Harriet admitted. She stared at Wilbur's wooden form.

"They aren't carvings, are they?" asked Ratpunzel.

"No," said Harriet. She felt very tired.

ALL THOSE PEOPLE WHO CAME TO TALK TO ME . . . MOTHER GOTHEL TRAPPED THEM ALL IN TREES, DIDN'T SHE?

"Yeah," said Harriet. She was tired and grumpy and would have said something sarcastic, like "Are you only now figuring that out?" but Wilbur wouldn't have wanted that. Wilbur would have been nice about it. Wilbur would have told her to be kind to Ratpunzel. And Ratpunzel had just saved her life, and that was pretty darn good for somebody who had been trapped in a tower all her life.

Think, Harriet! she thought, racking her brain. *Think! You're a hero! Use your brain!*

What had the book in Gothel's study said?

The tree shall hold them fast, and none shall be freed, even unto the end of the world . . .

Harriet slumped against the tree trunk.

"None shall be freed, even unto the end of the world . . ." she muttered out loud.

"No!" shouted Ratpunzel, practically in her ear.

"No! I won't let that happen! This isn't Sad Story Time! There's got to be a happy ending!"

She flung her arms around the wooden statue of Wilbur and burst into tears.

Harriet winced. She hated it when other people cried. She never knew what to say so they'd feel better. She wished Wilbur were here, and not a tree, so that he could deal with it. Wilbur could have patted Ratpunzel on the shoulder and said "There, there," and it would have meant something, because it was Wilbur saying it. When Harriet tried to say something comforting, it always came out wrong.

For some reason, "Don't cry! You've still got all your arms and legs! And nobody's on fire! That's something!" never went over well.

She felt, though she would never admit it, like crying herself.

And then, very faintly, Harriet heard a sound.

It sounded like ice breaking up on a river a long way away. It sounded like wood creaking in the wind.

It sounded a little bit like a hydra tapping at an eggshell.

CRACK!

Harriet looked up.

Ratpunzel was sobbing her heart out, and the tears were pouring over her fur and falling, one by one, onto the bark of the tree.

Had there been something else written in the book?

. . . none shall be freed, even unto the end of the world, except by the essence itself.

The essence in the tears! That's it! Gothel was making magic with the vials of tears, and she used them to lock all those people into trees, but Ratpunzel's crying tears now, real ones, onto the tree, and that's the essence.

Harriet held her breath. She didn't dare say a word, because if she was right and Ratpunzel stopped crying, Wilbur wouldn't be freed after all.

"You tried to save me!" wept Ratpunzel. "You were so n-nice and you listened and you told me about how y-y-you lived with your m-m-mom and you s-said I could come s-stay with you and . . ."

CRACK! CRACK!

It was louder now. Ratpunzel didn't seem to notice. Harriet watched as a bit of bark flaked off Wilbur's arm and warm, living fur showed underneath.

"And . . . and . . . I'm s-sorry . . . you should have left me . . . if you hadn't c-c-come to get me out of the tower, you w-would have gotten away . . ."

CRACK! CRACK!

Just a little more, thought Harriet, leaning forward. *Just a little bit more . . .*

"You were so brave!" cried Ratpunzel. "And I know you're a prince and when I grow up I want to marry you—"

Oh, ew, thought Harriet.

CRRRACK!

The tree split apart.
Wilbur fell out of
the tree and into
Harriet's arms.

CHAPTER 23

They handed the still-groggy Gothel over to the authorities in the Kingdom of Sunshine. The guards had been very firm but very cheerful.

WE'RE SURE SHE CAN BE REHABILITATED! WE'LL TEACH HER TO USE HER POWERS ONLY FOR THE GOODNESS AND HAPPINESS OF HER FELLOW CITIZENS!

AFTER A FEW YEARS IN OUR HAPPY HOSPITAL, SHE'LL BE A PRODUCTIVE MEMBER OF SOCIETY FOR SURE!

WE'LL TEACH HER TO WRITE POETRY ABOUT CLOUDS AND BABY BUNNIES AND TO SING "THE HAPPY BLUEBIRD IS SO HAPPY, HE MAKES ME HAPPY TOO!"

"And there will be Happy Story Time!" added another guard. "Stories where everyone holds hands and is the best person they can possibly be and everything is made of rainbows!"

Harriet almost felt a little sorry for Gothel. Almost.

When Mumfrey had finally returned, with the baby hydra strapped to his back, the hydra had promptly burst into tiny reptile tears. Harriet had been very worried, until they worked out that the hydra had loved going fast on quail-back, and was sad because the ride had stopped.

FASTER!

It took them nearly a week, using all the vials of tears stored up in Gothel's study, to free all the people trapped in trees. All the princes and warriors and strange beasts had been very happy to be freed.

A few swore allegiance to Harriet, which was sort of embarrassing. "No, no," she said. "I don't need your undying gratitude. No, nor eternal service either. No, I will *not* marry you! Definitely not! *I'm twelve!*"

Harriet saved the weasel-wolves for last, but when they saw Mumfrey and Harriet standing in front of the tree, with identical no-nonsense expressions, they weaseled hastily away into the forest.

Almost all the prisoners of the trees went home immediately to tell their families that they weren't dead, just . . . stuck. Only one stayed behind.

He was a handsome young rat prince, and Ratpunzel was very glad to see him.

Ratpunzel blushed. "Oh," she said. "Oh, dear. It's just . . . well . . . oh, I've promised to marry Wilbur, you see!" Her tail curled in embarrassment.

The rat prince frowned at Wilbur. "Must we fight a duel for the hand of fair Ratpunzel, then?"

NO! IT'S COOL! NOBODY NEEDS TO DUEL ANYBODY! WE WERE ALL A LITTLE OVERWROUGHT, THAT'S ALL!

To Harriet, he whispered, "Help me!"

Harriet sighed. "Sorry," she said to Ratpunzel. "Wilbur's already betrothed."

"To you?!" asked Ratpunzel.

"No! Jeez, you're as bad as my mother! No, to—uh—a very powerful—uh—warrior queen—from a different kingdom—"

"We've never met," put in Wilbur hastily. "It was arranged by our parents while we were still babies."

"Oh," said Ratpunzel. She sighed, partly with sadness, but also, Harriet thought, with relief.

OH! THEN I CAN MARRY THE RAT PRINCE!

PLEASE DO!

"Are you sure you wouldn't like to meet some other princes first?" asked Harriet. As much as she wanted to save Wilbur from untimely matrimony, she felt obligated to say something. "I mean, it's a big world, and you don't have to marry the first prince that comes to your tower . . . even if he's got a cast-iron stomach . . ."

Ratpunzel frowned, but the rat prince nodded to Harriet.

"I agree," he said. "This hamster is very wise. You should go with your friends. I shall come for you in a year, and if you still wish to marry me, then and only then shall we be wed!"

And he rode off in a cloud of dust, while Ratpunzel sighed after him.

ISN'T HE DREAMY?

Harriet rolled her eyes.

"Sure," she said. "If you like that sort of thing. Wilbur, why don't we take Ratpunzel to meet your mother—and our little hydra to meet *its* mother? I caught it trying to make a soufflé out of pine needles yesterday. It needs Heady to teach it what to do."

"That's a great plan," said Wilbur. "That is your best plan yet. And it doesn't even involve bungee cords."

"Well," said Harriet. "Not *yet*."

Ratpunzel climbed onto Mumfrey's back, behind Harriet. The hamster princess lifted the reins and clucked her tongue. "C'mon, Mumfrey. Let's go home."

ABOUT the AUTHOR

Ursula Vernon is an award-winning author and illustrator whose work has won a Hugo Award and a Nebula Award, and been nominated for the World Fantasy Award and an Eisner. She loves birding, gardening, and spunky heroines. She is the first to admit that she would make a terrible princess.